RETURN TO CAMP SOLGOHACHIA

THE RAVEN HILL BUTCHER BOOK TWO

Nasser Rabadi

ISBN: 978-1-954931-17-6

Also by Nasser Rabadi

THE RAVEN HILL BUTCHER slasher novel series

Book one: The Christmas Morning Massacre

Book two: Return to Camp Solgohachia

Book three: Noel Hell

Book four: The Curse of Raven Hill

Book five: The Final Chapter

Book six (reboot of Return to Camp Solgohachia): A New Beginning

Book seven (reboot of The Christmas Morning Massacre and Noel Hell): Winter Graves

Book eight: Santa's Space Station of Slaughter

Book nine: Santa Goes to Hell

Book ten: Into the Santa-Verse

The ENGSTROM HOUSE series

Book one: The Haunting of Engstrom House

Book two: Return to Engstrom House

Book three: The Curse of Engstrom House

DETECTIVE STARK'S STRANGE MYSTERIES series

NASSER RABADI

Book one: The Case of the Vanishing Blonde

Book two: The Case of the Cursed Carnival

Book three: The Case of the Haunted Insane Asylum

The AFTERLIFE series of psychological thrillers

Book one: Rough Cut

Book two: Kisses Can Kill

Book three: The Black Dress

Book four: Nightmare Town

Book five: That Old Black Magic

Book six: The Black Nightmare

Book seven: Red as Blood

Book eight: Dark Obsession

Contents

Chapter One

Raven Hill has always been an unlucky town.

The moon looks so out of place in daylight, Wesley Lawrence thought, looking through the bus window to the sky. He was reluctant to go back to Camp Solgohachia but all his friends were going so he figured why not. And now, as the bus went down the familiar bumpy road, he still regretted it. Wesley thought about all the things he'd rather be doing at home, like playing a video game or setting up glass bottles in the alley behind his house and seeing how far he could hit them with his slingshot.

Wesley's stomach dropped as the bus descended a steep slope. He hated that dropping feeling—that same feeling he would get when an elevator descended.

His friend Bill sat next to him, and his friend Darren was alone in the seat behind them—Darren was so fat he took up enough room for two campers. The rest of the bus was all neighborhood kids—most of them he knew but was not friends with.

It's going to be a fun two weeks, he thought. It always was. He was seventeen, and it was his fourth and final time at Camp Solgohachia, but camping was something he had outgrown. But at least there'd still be pranks and mayhem. He had his slingshot in his pocket and would surely launch rocks at the younger campers and first-timers.

WELCOME TO CAMP SOLGOHACHIA, the banner over the tall wooden entrance read, with SUMMER 1986 underneath it in smaller letters.

The driver parked in a big gravel parking lot, opened the door, and wished the kids fun times. Most of the luggage was piled into mountains in the back of the bus, and kids tackled each other to find their things so that they could get off and go into camp. Wesley, Bill, and Darren each kept their single bags at their feet so that they were the first ones off—Wesley was glad to finally stretch his legs. The ride was four hours with no stops and he had to pee from the two cans of Jolt Cola he downed within the first hour.

"Hurry up," Wesley said as Darren wobbled through the bus.

"I'm coming I'm coming."

Bill whistled and looked around. "It's burnin.'"

When Darren was out of the bus, the boys sped to a path on the right that went to the boys' cabins at the edge of the woods that hemmed around camp; the cabins stood on a slight rise. The girls' cabins were on the other side of camp.

The boys' cabins were named: Grizzly, Polar, Kodiak, Sun, and Panda. Grizzly was the first cabin, the most desirable one, and not technically a cabin. It was the only one with air conditioning and had nice tile floors and newly installed bathrooms.

"It must be taken already," Wesley said. "No way we made it in time."

"Definitely is." Bill pointed his thumb. "Somebody already put a garbage can outside. Look."

RETURN TO CAMP SOLGOHACHIA

Putting a garbage can outside the door was tradition amongst the boys at Camp Solgohachia to let the later arrivals know a cabin was full.

"Well kill me if we've gotta be stuck in Panda."

"Panda isn't so bad," Darren said. "It may be ugly and falling apart but it's not so bad."

"The toilets in Panda don't even flush! And look how the trees almost grow *into* it, I bet it's swarming with bugs."

Polar was next on the path of cabins and was the next most desirable, but that too had a garbage can in front of it. So did Brown, Kodiak, and Sun.

The boys stopped in front of Panda; its name was painted in wobbly red letters, and the green paintjob on the cabin was chipping away. The branches of giant trees covered it and almost formed a second roof. Somewhere in the distance bees hummed, and Wesley hoped they wouldn't have to deal with bees or any type of bug with a stinger for the next couple weeks.

"Panda it is, I guess," Wesley reached for the knob. "I had Grizzly my first year, right after they fixed it up. Man I wish all cabins were like that. Had all sorts of bragging rights that year…"

"I remember when you showed me inside," Bill said. "Sure was nice."

"Maybe Panda won't be so bad," Darren pushed his crooked glasses up."

Nobody else was in Panda; they had it all to themselves.

The cabin stunk but it was unclear where the stench was coming from. The bunkbeds were high off the ground, and were old and rickety, as if they hadn't been replaced since the place opened in the

NASSER RABADI

1930s. At least the blue covers over the musty grey mattresses were new; but they didn't have bedsheets, and there was no way Wesley was touching that with his body. Tall dressers were set between the bunks, and there were some other dressers at one end. The floor creaked with every step.

Wesley tossed his bag atop the high bunk in the far left corner with the window facing camp. "Dibs."

He climbed the ladder then studied the beams that raced across the ceiling. Often times the boys had races with these, seeing who could climb to the other end and back first. Wesley thought that if anyone tried that in Panda, that roof would surely collapse. Wesley put his hands to it anyways and searched around the beams for treasure but only found dust; he had been lucky once and found a silver dollar on a beam, but he hadn't been lucky since.

Bill tossed his bag on the bunk below Wesley's, and Darren took the bottom bunk next to Bill.

A whisper of cold came when Wesley opened the door to leave the cabin. He looked up to see the clouds covering the sun, then turned back to his friends who were still loading their clothes into dresser drawers.

"Come on, fruitcakes."

Clouds moved away from the sun and the temperature rose. The boys went to the flagpole at the center of camp; all the boys and girls of Camp Solgohachia were heading there for morning announcements.

The flagpole was probably twenty feet high and danced in the wind. A man stood on the bricks that ran in circles around the pole and the flowers that grew around it.

"Goooooood morning campers! I'm your camp director Charlie and welcome to Camp Solgohachia, summer of 1986! I know a lot of you have been here before and know the spiel but listen up! It's time to go over some camp rules before we get things started! Now let's see a show of hands, who has *never* been camping before?"

Plenty of campers, mostly the younger kids, raised their hands.

"And who's been camping before but never been to Camp Solgohachia before?"

Some others raised their hands.

"Well it's a pleasure to have you all here! This is going to be the best summer yet! I'll need you kids to pay attention and save all questions for the end. We have five very special rules we ask you all to follow at Camp Solgohachia. The first is to be a happy camper! Be kind to everyone. No name calling, bullying, or fighting. The second rule is to listen to your counselor. Every cabin will soon be assigned their own counselor. Camp counselors are there to make sure that all campers have the best time possible while also looking out for every camper's safety. Listen to them. Third is to keep the camp and cabins clean! Four is to have fun! Make new friends and try new things. You'll make friendships here that can last lifetimes, I know I sure did when I was a camper! Now, the fifth and final rule is the absolute most important. *Do. Not. Go. Out. After. Curfew.* Once we hit the twilight period, the period before our evening events, there is absolutely *no* wandering alone, always accompany a friend. After that is curfew, and there is absolutely no sneaking out. Every year we have kids who try to break into the boarded cabin through the east end of the woods—this is absolutely frowned upon, and that area of the woods is off limits. Any camper found going there will have to clean the latrine and have privileges taken away. Is that understood?"

Wesley pulled his buddies to the side. "Guys?"

"Yeah?"

"It's our last year here. What if we went to that cabin? See what all the fuss is about?"

"Go to the cabin?" Darren gulped. *"Go to the cabin!?!?"*

"Shut up, not so loud," Wesley said. "Yes, go to the cabin. It sounds like fun. What're they gonna do? Send me home? I didn't wanna come this year anyways. Look, nothing's gonna happen, it's all just some story to scare campers with."

"Definitely made up," bill said. "Bet you won't go anyways though."

"Would too."

"Whoever sneaks over first is the winner?"

Wesley stuck out his hand; Bill shook it. "It's a deal."

Chapter Two

When Charlie was done speaking the campers were free to wander around and do as they pleased; there were no scheduled activities on the first day. The sun was blazing and it must have been touching ninety degrees. There was much to do: baseball, basketball, human foosball, golf, water balloon volleyball, and carpetball. Carpetball was played under a ramada with vending machines and tables, and was where Wesley sat with his eyes on a blondie wearing a denim skirt and tight pink shirt.

Wesley sat crouched over the edge of the table with his hands and slingshot under it, and a stack of pebbles hidden at his side. He slipped one into the leather pad on the rubber and winded it back; it hit a boy of thirteen or fourteen in the calf. Wesley laughed watching the boy grab his leg on the brink of tears—what a baby.

Wesley looked away, and when nobody fessed up, the boy tried to go back to carpetball. Wesley hit him again; everyone laughed at his painful reaction. Nobody saw who had shot him. Nobody, of course, except the blondie.

After the third time he hit the boy, Blondie came over and said, "You're a real jerk you know."

NASSER RABADI

"What?"

"I saw you throwing rocks at that boy."

"It's just a little prank."

"Whatever."

"I'm Wesley, what's your name?"

"You wish." Blondie upturned her nose then left the ramada and went off into camp.

Wesley stood up from the bench and tripped onto the cement floor; he got to his feet and hurried after her. *"Hey wait up."*

She turned around confused. "What do you want?"

"I've never seen you around before. You new here?"

Blondie eyed the slingshot Wesley was clutching. "You gonna shoot me with that thing too, huh?"

"What?" He looked down at his hands then stuffed the slingshot into his pocket. "No—no I'm not. I was just having fun with that kid. Just a camp prank."

She turned and walked away.

"I'm sorry I hit that kid. Let me make it up to you. Can I buy you an ice cream cone?"

Blondie stopped, wiped her hair from her eyes, then turned back to him. "My name's Wendy. And yes, I am new here."

"You just move to Raven Hill?"

"Yep."

"This is my fourth year at camp. Mind if I show you around?"

"As long as you don't fling any rocks at me."

"I won't as long as you behave yourself, Wendy."

He took her off the path and through the grass as a shortcut; next to the carpetball armada was the open area behind the cafeteria and

8

before the start of the golf fields; it was on a rise, an area not typically traveled since there was nothing there. The back of the cafeteria had a porch that nobody usually used; below it was an open hiding space that—as far as he knew—no one else knew about.

"You can hide here."

"Hide here?"

"You know, if you ever want to skip out on activities."

"Why's the first place you show me a hiding spot?"

Wesley pointed to the right. "Well we were pretty close. Over there's golf. This is the cafeteria. The line can be a pain, I'd say get there as early as you can."

"That's common sense. What else is there to do around here?"

He led her back to the path; it curved into the camp. "Well back around here are the basketball courts. That building right next to it has postcards and candy and stuff you can buy. And a payphone in the back."

Wendy turned towards the basketball hoops and watched people play.

"You know anyone playing?"

"No," Wendy said in a low voice. Her face turned red. "I don't know anybody here."

"You like basketball?"

"I love it."

"You should teach me sometime," Wesley said. "Come on, this way."

Wendy followed him; she glimpsed behind her shoulder at the basketball courts a couple times. "Thank you for showing me around."

"I'm surprised a pretty girl like you doesn't know anyone here. What made you come to Camp Solgohachia?"

"Mom and Dad thought it'd help me meet more kids from town."

"Where you from?"

"Radley," she said. "Far away in Radley."

"Maybe we could hang out after this. You know, after camp, back in Raven Hill."

"Maybe."

"Well down that way's the swim hole, past the boys' cabins. I'm down in the last one. And over there by the girls' cabins," he pointed in the totally opposite direction, "when they go on hiking trips, they usually go over a mountain down that way, but I've never gone on one."

"Thanks for showing me around," Wendy said then walked away. "I think I'm going to the basketball courts."

"See you around?"

"I think so. This place isn't *that* big."

Wesley watched her walk away. She was prettier than all the other girls at camp. He wondered if she lived close to him—unlike camp, Raven Hill *was* a big place.

Wesley found one of the coolers of ice water that were placed around camp, and filled a paper cup; it was refreshing. A few minutes later Wesley took his slingshot out and went back to the armada, grabbed handfuls of pebbles, and sat back alone at the bench. He wondered what Bill and Darren were up to right now; he hadn't seen them in a while.

He looked around for the boy he had hit last time—it would be hilarious to see him squirm again—but couldn't find him. Instead, he launched his rocks at a new target: another boy in shorts watching an intense game of carpetball, cheering every time the guy in the green shirt knocked over the pool balls of the guy in the *Led Zeppelin* shirt.

Wesley fired a pebble at the boy's shoulder—the boy nearly jumped over the table when he felt it hit him. The boy turned around; his face white under freckles, and turning to anger. Wesley secretly launched another from under the table and it hit the boy in the stomach. Wesley looked away quickly, bursting out in laughter, and the boy looked around the crowded armada wondering who the hell could've been throwing rocks at him.

Camp is gonna be just fine after all, Wesley thought.

Chapter Three

Wesley, Bill, and Darren were some of the first ones to line up for dinner in front of the cafeteria; Wesley kept an eye out for Wendy but didn't see any sign of her—she could've been anywhere, and with the amount of kids here—Wesley figured there were well over one hundred—it was easy to lose track of somebody.

"Could you believe it?" Darren asked. "Really, could you guys believe it? Playing baseball in this weather? I almost fainted I tell you. *Fainted.* They laughed at me when I asked to pause for a water break."

"Calm it, tits," Wesley said. "I'm sure it was so exhausting striking out every single time you were at bat."

"*I got on base once.* I was hit by a pitch, but I still go ton base…"

"Come on, move already," Bill said.

Then, as if at his command, the front doors opened and the line got to moving.

The camp served pizza today as they always did on the first and last days. Technically not camp food, and it was delicious—one of the only two or three days when the food they served was good.

NASSER RABADI

Wesley was not looking forward to awful "Bean Surprise" for lunch tomorrow or roasting doughboys over the fire tonight. Wesley wondered if Mom and Dad would send a care package this year—usually they sent snacks, cookies, things he'd actually enjoy eating. He'd probably be down twenty pounds after the two weeks here, with how little of camp's food was tolerable.

Wesley and his friends sat at the end of a crowded table near a window. Wesley sipped lemonade then ate his bag of chips first.

"You'll never believe what happened to me guys. I met the most beautiful girl today, her name's Wendy and she's new around here. I' gonna sit by her at the bonfire tonight."

"How do you plan to pry her away from her friends?" Darren asked.

"That's the thing—she has none. She let me show her around. She knows nobody. She's new. Isn't that great?"

Darren and Bill looked at each other, then back to Wesley and laughed.

"What's so funny?"

"Oh my God, Wes," Bill said, "don't you know this already? If a pretty girl has no friends it's usually because she's a bitch. Everyone wants to be friends with a pretty girl."

"She's not a bitch, she's nice."

"That's the Tic Tac between your legs talking," Darren said. "You've barely met her. She *has* to be a piece of—"

"You guys'll meet her tonight, but don't embarrass me."

"We definitely won't embarrass you," Bill said. "Maybe you should try taking her to that boarded up cabin."

"Oh yeah, are still up for our little bet, Bill?"

RETURN TO CAMP SOLGOHACHIA

"Definitely. Are you? Maybe after the bonfire?"

"Yeah dude."

Darren took a bite of his pizza then spit it out. *Too hot! Too hot! Oh God did Satan heat this thing? My tongue!*

Darren picked up the piece he spat out and ate it.

"Gross," Wesley said. "You're gonna make me sick."

A little later after eating, it was time to swim, so the boys walked back to the cabin for their trunks. The weather cooled; soft breezes whistled through the trees and fell over Camp Solgohachia. The clouds were low and thick.

Hair clung to Wesley's face; he moved it away but it only fell back in place and became stuck again with hot sweat trickling down his face. At least he couldn't hear bees humming anymore—that was a great thing, because bees were his biggest fear. When he had been a little boy, about five or six, and fishing with his dad, his uncle, and his cousins, he ran barefoot through the grass surrounding the lake and stepped on a bee that stung his foot. It was the most pain Wesley had ever felt in his life.

Out of fear he glanced down real quick to make sure there were no bees in the grass before the cabin, then walked into Panda. There were three other campers in bunks and filling up dresser drawers and changing into trunks, and a counselor who sat on a bottom bunk closest to the door and was all ready to go to the swim hole.

NASSER RABADI

"Hello," the counselor said in an overly happy voice, a voice that Wesley thought the counselors were all forced into faking. "I'm Vince, I'm your cabin's counselor. Have you guys been having a great first day?"

"Yeah," Wesley said. Then he added: "I'm Wesley. Tall one's Bill, tits is Darren."

"Come on, that's not a nice way to talk about your bunkmate."

"No, no, it's fine. Really," Darren said. "I'm used to it."

The boy in blue trunks and a blue shirt said, "I'm Al."

"Pleasure to meet yas. I'm Chester," the redhead said.

"Ralph," the short one mumbled.

"I'm heading to the swim hole now," Vince said. "See you guys there."

Vince shut the door behind himself.

"Man, what a fairy," Wesley said.

"For sure," Bill said.

Al laughed. "Yeah you're probably right."

"Hey, let me ask you new guys a question," Wesley said. "You meet a hot girl, she's new here, she's got no friends. What's it mean?"

"Easy," Chester said, "she's a bitch. Every hot girl without friends must be one or she'd have friends. Everyone wants ta be friends with a hot girl."

"Even if she's new?"

"Especially if she's new," Al said. "What, you think she's walking around here without anyone noticing? Every guy wants to show the new girl around, show her a good time, and every chick wants a new friend to talk about behind their backs."

"Well she didn't seem like a bitch when I talked to her…"

RETURN TO CAMP SOLGOHACHIA

"Who is she?" Al asked.

"Wendy. We talked for a few minutes, I swear she isn't a bit—"

"Wendy… Wendy…" Chester said. "Doesn't ring a bell."

"Heh, we tried to tell him," Darren said. "We *tried* to tell him. But ole Wes here doesn't listen. Oh boy, he wants to learn the hard way."

"Oh come on you guys haven't met her. I'm gonna bring her around to the bonfire tonight, then you'll see."

While Wesley, Bill, and Darren changed into their trunks, Al, Chester, and Ralph left for the swim hole.

Wesley wondered if his friends were right. Was she as bad as everyone thought? He didn't think so. She was new, she didn't have time yet to meet people. After all, it isn't as if friendships are formed in five minutes. Wesley lived next door to Darren and it took them years before they became friends at all.

What do these guys know anyways? They're wrong.

The swim hole was a giant in-ground circle of murky green-blue water divided in half by a yellow fence. On one side—the shallow side, which anybody could use—was a volleyball net, a small slide, and two low basketball hoops with green and white striped basketballs. On the other end—the deep end, which you'd have to pass a swimming test to use—was a bigger slide, a wooden deck, and *the blob.*

The blob was a giant yellow and blue inflatable structure that required two people to use; one person—usually the smaller of the two—would jump from the deck to the blob and sit on the far end of it. The other person—the bigger of the two—would then jump straight down from the deck, causing the smaller person to go flying through the air then landing into the water.

Once and only once had someone hit the fence in the whole history of the camp—the fence was very far from the blob, and the person who launched that person into the fence had been very fat. Luckily that kid wasn't hurt so badly—he came away with a few bruises. It could've been much worse if he had landed differently.

Wesley kicked off his flipflops and ran down to the far end, where he waited in one of two lines for his turn to take the swim test. The test was simple, and he passed every year: swimming down to the other end and back.

When his turn came he jumped in and swam; something about the motion was just natural to him. The water was lukewarm, a little on the cold side, but he hit a warm pocket and went to the other end as fast as he could. When he made it there, he touched the concrete edge, glanced quickly around to see if Wendy was there, didn't see her, turned around and swam back. Down at the end he was returning to, he saw Bill and Al and Chester in line; he didn't know if Ralph swam but he knew Darren couldn't, and soon he'd be dunking Darren under water.

But for now: the blob.

He raced up the wooden steps; the wait for the blob wasn't long, it went fairly quickly. Launching a guy into the air wasn't a long process. Wesley's turn came and he jumped off the platform—it must've been about ten feet high if he had to guess—then crawled to the edge. He prepared himself for liftoff, turned around, gave the tubby dude on the platform a thumbs up.

"Ready."

Wesley turned back and by the time he was looking forward he was already in the air. There was a loud *SMACK!* of the guy slamming into the blob then everything became a blur—the world rushed by and he had that thrill of falling—limbs flailing, mouth agape but shutting as he realized he was coming down face-first into water. He splashed under the green-blue chilly surface then rose with his hair plastered to his face and big smile running across his thin lips.

"That was awesome dude," Wesley said, then noticed the fat man who blobbed him was about to be blobbed by an even bigger man. Wesley put his arms around the yellow fence then watched the fatty climb into the sky, panic on his face—he must not have been blobbed often—and come crashing like a cannonball not far from Wesley.

The man resurfaced. *"Woah mama that was fun."*

Wesley swam back to the wooden deck and went back up the dripping wet stairs, grabbing the railing tight, went back in line—longer now than it had been the first time—and waited in line behind a girl. From his place up top on the deck he could see most of the swim hole—although most people on the shallow end were just dots from up here—and tried to find Wendy. At first he looked for a girl in a denim skirt and a tight pink shirt, then he thought, *She wouldn't have worn that to swim in.*

The line moved fast and when it was Wesley's turn again he was blobbed by an even bigger guy than the first time, and was flung so far he almost became the second person in history to hit the fence that divided the deep end and the shallow end. For a moment he was suspended in air, and all he saw was yellow. Even as he shut his eyes he saw the bar coming closer and closer, tried to somehow push his body away from it, and landed on his back in the water just a foot away from the fence. When he resurfaced he heard many people gasping and laughing.

After that, he decided it was time to head over to the shallow end and see what was going on. Darren and Ralph were chilling against the fence, hardly waist-deep in the swim hole. Bill, Al, Chester, and some other boys were playing basketball on one hoop while some girls were playing basketball on the other. He thought for sure Wendy would be playing with the girls—she had said she liked basketball—but she wasn't there.

Wesley snuck through the game of basketball, put Bill in a choke hold—which was difficult since Bill was much taller—then dragged him under the water and let go. Bill resurfaced, grabbed Wesley, lifted him up, then dropped him in the water with a big splash.

The game of basketball abruptly ended and suddenly everybody was dunking everybody. Chester dunked Al, Al dunked a random bald boy, somebody Wesley couldn't see dunked him. When Wesley came back up he saw that Darren and Ralph hadn't seen the dunking party going on because they were watching the blobbing going on.

"Hey, over there." Wesley pointed. "Let's get them."

Wesley and Al crept over to their unsuspecting friends, then Wesley put his arm around Darren, and Al helped grab him too.

"Oh what is this what are you guys doing don't dunk me don't dunk me please."

"Everybody gets at least one," Wesley said.

Al turned back to Ralph. "What he said. Yer next, Ralphie."

RETURN TO CAMP SOLGOHACHIA

Ralph was frozen with terror.

Darren tried to wiggle free. *"But I can't swim I don't know what to do what do I do? Please—"*

"Just plug your nose," Al said.

Darren slipped an arm free from Wesley. He started to ask, as he raised his hand to his face, "Like this—" but before he could reach his nose, they let go of him and he went under three feet of water. A moment later he came to the surface thrashing his arms around as if the shark from *Jaws* were after him.

"I'm drowning I'm drowning oh God this is the end! Goodbye cruel world!"

Bill grabbed him by the shoulders. "Get ahold of yourself, you're standing up dude."

"Huh? I am?"

Darren looked down and wrinkled his nose. "I swallowed some of it! Some of it went in my nose! It hurts! Oh God, you know what kind of diseases could be in this water?"

"None of us have aids," Wesley said.

Al looked back at Ralph who was climbing out of the water. "Your turn Ralphie."

"Come on, Al, no."

That was the most Wesley had heard Ralph speak yet. He was a quiet boy—short and thin. He looked like a small frightened child the way he backed away from Al. There were almost tears in his eyes.

"I hate the water. Come on please no."

Wesley laughed. He was like Darren's skinny twin.

He watched Al pull Ralph back into the water and toss him down. Ralph jerked and squirmed and reached for something to grab onto as he sank. It was funny to watch, but Wesley felt bad for him and reached down to help him up. Back on the surface, Ralph spat out a mouthful of water and coughed uncontrollably. Al walloped his hand on Ralph's back to help him spit the water up, but very little came out.

"Sorry, 'cuz," Al said.

"You're cousins?"

"Yep."

One of the basketballs drifted near Wesley; he grabbed it, looked at all the guys who had been playing a few minutes ago, then asked, "Can one of you guys show me how to throw this thing?"

Bill grabbed it from his hands then demonstrated. "Like this, Wes, rest it on the tips of your right fingers like this. Left hand on the side. Just flick your wrist."

Bill took a shot for example; it hit the backboard and went in. A stranger grabbed it from under the hoop and tossed it back to Bill. Bill handed it to Wesley, then Wesley tried to shoot. It clanged off the front of the rim and splashed five feet away.

"It'll be easier on land," Bill said.

Wesley grabbed the ball again and took a shot from the left of the hoop. Backboard. Far right rim. Bound to the end of the swim hole by the concrete edge.

"You'll get the hang of it," Chester said, grabbed it, then waddled to the hoop for a dunk. "Must be what Kareem Abdul-Jabbar feels like."

Chester reached for the ball, then Darren of all people grabbed hold of him and dunked him under water. Chester resurfaced and splashed handfuls of water at Darren; Darren flinched, turned away, and flopped face-first into the water and squirmed. The boys laughed then Ralph helped him out.

Clouds ripped away from the sun and it was bright again; the water was heating up and the occasional breeze swung by. Somebody dunked Wesley again, then Wesley dunked Al, and there was another round of dunking everybody before a shootaround on the hoops. A few shots later, Wesley finally made one. It was probably one make out of fifteen tries, but at least he made it. Time was flying by, and he went to the blob one last time before some of the counselors announced swim time was over.

Chapter Four

The sun was sinking. Tints of orange mixed with shades of red and tones of purple across the wide fading hues of rich blue sky over Camp Solgohachia. Everyone was leaving the swim hole. Cool breezes swept over them.

Wesley yawned and dried himself with his towel and went back to Panda. He wondered what Mom and Dad and his sister Sadie and his dog Doug were up to right now. He didn't know what time it was but figured Dad was portably home from work by now, dinner was probably ready, and Mom was yelling at the dog to get away from the table. She might've been serving fried chicken or steak—something the dog couldn't resist at all—and if he had been home, he'd secretly have given pieces of it to his pet.

In Panda, the boys showered; there were three separate showers, and Wesley, Bill, and Darren were first since they had arrived at the cabin first today and therefore had dibs on first showers. The water was hot and relaxing, and Wesley didn't want to leave.

"Ahhhhhh!"

Wesley turned sharply. "Darren?"

RETURN TO CAMP SOLGOHACHIA

Darren screamed. *"Give me back my clothes oh God my towel too! They took my towel too! Come on guys how will I get out of here?"*

Their bunkmates were laughing, and Wesley couldn't help but join in—Bill too. When Wesley was done, he dried off in the stall then dressed up, and leaving the shower, Darren was still screaming for his clothes.

"Come on guys," Wesley said. "Let's give him back his things."

Chester grabbed his can of shaving cream from the counter. "We're just gettin started, ya see?"

"Take it easy on him."

Chester didn't listen; he crept up to the stall, put his hand over the railing, then sprayed shaving cream all over Darren.

"Oh my God." Darren screamed as if he were being stabbed.

"It's just shaving cream is all," Bill said. "Chill out Darren, we'll get you your clothes now."

Al tossed the towel over the railing. "Here dude."

"Thank you," Darren said on the brink of tears. "My clothes? Where are my clothes?"

Chester rolled them up then tossed them into the shower like a basketball. *"Threeeee pointerrrr."*

"They're wet! They're all wet! How am I supposed to dress in these? You ever dress in wet clothes? They don't fit right!"

Wesley looked in the mirror. He made sure none of his dog's hair was on his jeans or his red polo—Doug's hair seemed to travel with him everywhere he went. Wesley brushed his teeth, then laid down on his bunk and shut his eyes for a minute. There was a little time to kill since the other boys were just getting started with their showers and they were all gonna leave at the same time.

"Don't fall asleep," Bill said.

"Just shuttin' my eyes until we head out. Besides, hard enough to sleep with Darren over there sniffling in the corner."

"I'm not crying."

It had been a tiring and fun day.

Wesley did almost sleep; he was on the brink of passing out when Al, Ralph, and Chester were all done showering then changing into new outfits.

Bill shook him. "Wake up. Bonfire time."

Darren was complaining again: *"These guys took my towel they threw my clothes into the water, what's next? They're gonna throw me into the bonfire?"*

"Oh quit it," Al said then whipped him with a towel. "Only a camp prank is all. Loosen up."

"Ouch."

Wesley hopped down from his bunk and put on his shoes, then all the boys from Panda headed out for the bonfires and food—if it could even be called that. The food that camp served at the bonfires was crud. But the campers would eat it anyways. Dough-boys—dough roasted over fire on a stick—without any sauce or cheese to dip it in, smores made of cheap marshmallows and generic gram crackers with Hersey bars that are already half melted, and sometimes unsalted sunflower seeds.

Camp Solgohachia didn't have one big fire—there were too many campers for that. Instead they had several small ones set around camp. Logs burned surrounded by even bigger logs used as seats. And now that it had gotten even darker outside while the boys had showered, the lights of the distant fires were the only things to guide them off the path from Panda and the other cabins down into camp.

"How do they expect us to see without lights?" Darren said. "I could fall here and twist my ankle! This is—this is insane! Do they think I have night vision? Oh this is dangerous! Very dangerous!"

"Sit on it," Chester said.

The boys went around the camp looking for an empty fire, and found one just off the basketball courts. There were boxes of smores ingredients, dough, green sticks, packs of unsalted seeds.

"Where's that broad of yours?" Al asked.

"I don't know," Wesley said. "Haven't seen her since this morning."

"Maybe she was a ghost," Darren said. "Oh man I should've known that our last year here we'd be haunted! Wesley finding a girl was too good to be true!"

"There's something much worse you have to worry about here than ghosts," Al said. "Don't you know?"

"Worse?"

Ralph gulped. "What's worse than ghosts?"

"Hold on," Wesley said then walked away. "I think I might know where she is. I'll be right back."

"Oh no where are you going? Don't go into the dark! Wesley! Oh man it was nice knowing you!"

"He'll be fine, buddy," Bill said.

Wesley entered dense darkness and about twenty feet ahead he went past the carpetball armada and behind the cafeteria to the lit back deck. No counselors were around to see him sneaking back here. He had no clue if Wendy was here or not, but it was worth a shot.

NASSER RABADI

He reached for his pocket, forgetting he had left his flashlight in his bag. "Wendy?"

The hiding area he showed her was draped in darkness and hidden from the naked eye. "Wendy it's Wesley. You hiding there?"

He came within five feet of it when she came out of the darkness.

"What're you doing here Wendy?" Her lovely blonde hair was parted down the middle, and she wore a long red skirt and a black and white striped long sleeve shirt.

"I was looking for you, I thought maybe you'd come by here."

"Oh, I was looking for you too. Come meet my friends at our fire. Your cabinmates didn't take you to theirs?"

"No they… left without me."

"Forget about them."

Wendy nodded and went with Wesley.

"Were you hiding here too during swim time?"

"What? No, I was at the swim hole."

"You were? I didn't see you at all. And I was looking for you."

"Glad my face is memorable."

"Hey, I didn't mean that your face wasn't memor—"

"I know, I'm joking," she smiled. "Thank you Wes. Thanks for being so nice to me."

"You're welcome. And thanks for behaving. Here I thought I'd have to hit you with the slingshot."

"If you did that, I'd never talk to you again."

"You know, we should exchange addresses Wendy. So when we get back to Raven—"

"There he is!" Darren screamed. *"Wes, you're alive!"*

RETURN TO CAMP SOLGOHACHIA

"Of course I'm alive," Wesley said, and he and Wendy came close to the fire. "So like I was saying, when we get back to Raven Hi—"

"Who's this beauty?" Bill asked.

They were at the fire now. "Guys this is Wendy. Wendy, meet Bill, Darren, over there's Al, his cousin Ralph, and Chester."

"Nice to meet you all," she said.

Wendy and Wesley sat next to each other in the last open spots.

Under the dark sky devoid of clouds, and scattered with stars many lightyears away, they passed around the sticks and marshmallows and dough. Wesley roasted a doughboy while everyone else went for marshmallows.

"Ya know, Darren thought you were a ghost, Wendy," Chester said.

Wendy looked at Darren. "Boo."

"Didn't you say, Al, there was something worse than guh-guh-ghosts?" Darren asked.

Al's expression became serious; he did not blink. Flames flickered and shadows moved along his face. He said, "The murders weren't very far from Camp Solgohachia... I'm gonna give it to you straight—he's still out there, The Raven Hill Butcher was never found. Raven Hill is jinxed."

"Yeah right," Wendy said.

"Some folks have claimed to see him in this very camp."

"None of that is true, it's another boogeyman to scare kids with."

"Didn't you know why he killed them?"

Wendy gulped and leaned forward. "No."

"Legend has it—"

"Ah!" Wendy screamed; Wesley had put his hands on her shoulders, making her jump. Wendy gave him a nasty look. "Stop that," she said, then looked back at Al, the only boy who wasn't laughing at her. She asked, "You mean those girls who died like fifteen years ago?"

"Right. My older brother told me all about it. You know that boarded up cabin the counselors tell you to stay away from? There's a reason it's boarded up. It belonged to that guy who killed those girls, and legend has it if you go to the cabin, he'll find you."

"Then why isn't it demolished?" Wendy asked.

"Like that would stop him," Al said. "He'd come for the campers anyways."

Everyone went silent; embers rose from the fire then fizzled out.

Al said, "If he catches you… it's not worth thinkin about."

"No, come on, tell us," Wesley said. "I love a good horror story around a campfire. Nobody's ever told me one this good before."

But then he shuddered; even under the heat of the fire, he shuddered. Part of it had to be true, and that was awful. What really did happen to those girls? What really did happen to that man who killed them? Would anyone ever have all of the answers?

"Once he has his eyes set on you, there's no escape. Those girls tried to escape. Hell, they had head starts. But The Butcher… he's not human. Not anymore."

"You're—you're scaring me man," Darren said.

"Quit it Darren," Bill said.

Darren stuffed his face with a smore.

"If you think those girls were random targets, think again," Al said with a dreadful grin of terror.

"What—what is he?" Ralph asked. "Why isn't he human?"

RETURN TO CAMP SOLGOHACHIA

"Because he was dead, and their belief in him brought him back to life. Their fears brought him back, and," his voice became a hush, much lower than a whisper, "he kills those who are most frightened."

"None of that can be true, things like that don't happen," Wendy said.

"Wendy, it's just a story, we know that," Wesley said. "That's the point of these things. To be scared. We know it can't happen."

"I'd be much more scared if I knew it was something *real,* Wes. Not boogeymen."

"Okay, I know," Wesley said. Everybody turned their attention to Wesley. He finished his doughboy, put a marshmallow on the stick, roasted it, then continued: "It happened in a place called Lilly Grove. The Redhead Murders. This guy—some author—figured it out but I hear now he's a hermit living in God-knows-where."

"Wuh-what happened?" Ralph asked.

"Think I heard of that," Chester said. "His own sister was one of 'em, right? I seen her picture in the newspaper. Absolutely smokin'."

"She was," Wesley said. "Before she was tortured. There were ten or eleven other women, each found mostly nude and some with burns."

"There are some *sick* people in the world," Wendy said.

"Not as sick as The Butcher," Al said. "I'd watch my back if I were you. He's got a thing for pretty girls."

"Knock it off," Wesley said.

"It's true. They were pretty girls, hair parted down the middle just like hers. Gutted, heads severed, and—"

"It's called tact, Al."

"My brother told me about a girl who died here when he was a camper. Do you wanna hear it?"

"Someone died here?" Ralph asked.

"Does he only kill girls? Am I safe?" Darren asked.

"Nobody's safe."

"I wanna hear," Chester said.

"Tell us," Bill said.

Al cleared his throat. "There was a girl one night who was dared to sneak out to the cabin, so she left after the counselor fell asleep. Now her bunkmates all watched her from the windows until she was out of sight. Then there was a long period of silence before they heard her screaming bloody murder. It was so loud when it woke up their counselor, the girls all acted like they didn't know what was going on… and their counselor ran outside with a flashlight. You know what she found?"

Everybody was still.

"Blood drizzled over tree branches. Pieces of skin hanging like fruit between the leaves. And about a mile into the woods, they found her head. The rest of her body was never found."

"Enough! Enough! I can't take it anymore! I can't take it!"

Everybody laughed at Darren.

"Relax," Chester said. "Life's no fun bein' serious all the time."

Wesley noticed Wendy was breathing shallowly. She must've been scared too. Wesley couldn't tell why she would be—it was all tall tales. He had heard many, many different legends about The Raven Hill Butcher, and he could probably tell them ten different versions that directly contradicted what Al was saying. He didn't want to—it would've made Darren and Ralph less scared when they finally realized it was a lark. Imagination. Nothing more than fables.

Wesley had heard all sorts of things, from the two dead girls having been part of cults, to drug deals gone wrong, to all sorts of stories about affairs. The speculation was endless. But there was one thing he couldn't knock from his mind: he was actually scared of The Raven Hill Butcher. He kept that to himself—Al's stories did not scare him, but he was scared of the real man.

Somebody had butchered those two girls before there was even some sort of Butcher to believe in. In his mind, The Raven Hill Butcher was some sort of shadow creature, some sort of man comprised entirely of shadows, with an old rusty—yet sharp—knife that is an extension of himself. An extension of The Butcher. And it could never be separated from him. No matter how much someone would try to fight back—there'd be no escaping.

"You know," Wesley said, "one of my uncles once tried to scare me with a story about The Butcher when I wouldn't go to bed one night. Eventually, when I did go to bed, and the lights were off, and very little light—if any—came through my window… in the corner of my room I thought I saw him watching me. And all night I was still. I probably laid there for hours trying not to make a movement or noise until I finally fell asleep, hoping he'd think I was already dead and that he'd go off to find another little kid. I was ten, could you blame me? But the shapes I saw in my room always stayed in my mind. The look he had. I started to dream about him. those didn't last long. But whenever I thought of him, he was always those shapes."

"Solid black?" Al said. "All one solid mass."

"Yes, exactly like that, exactly like a man who was only shadow."

"That's how I picture him too."

"And me," Bill said.

"Suh-same," Darren said.

So did Ralph, Chester, and Wendy. Everybody agreed that The Raven Hill Butcher took form as a black mass in their minds.

And suddenly Wesley's stomach turned.

Hypnotizing cold came over Camp Solgohachia, almost blowing out their fire.

"It doesn't mean anything right?" Ralph asked. "That we see him… the same."

"No," Wendy said. "A shadow's an easy thing to picture."

"I think I've had just about enough of this," Darren said. "If we keep talking about him I'm leaving."

"How are you guys liking the doughboys and smores?" Wesley asked.

"Garbage as always," Al said. "I'd kill for pizza again. It's gonna be a long two week til we get decent food around here."

"Tell me about it," Wesley said. "I brought a pack of Oreos with me but those were all finished as soon as the bus drove away. Man I miss good food."

"I wonder if the counselors get pizza whenever they want," Darren said. "I can almost still taste it, the cheese—oh God, the cheese."

"Hey Wes," Bill said, "we still on for our little bet?"

"Oh, um…"

"What bet?" Wendy asked.

"Havin a little race seeing who'll get to the boarded up cabin first. We talked about it this morning at the flagpole."

"Um, I don't know, Bill, it's getting late."

RETURN TO CAMP SOLGOHACHIA

"You scared?" Al asked.

"I'm not scared. But everybody's out tonight for the bonfires and it... I don't know, are we gonna get away from Vince? Sneak out while he's asleep? Seems easier during the day."

Chester laughed. "It'll be a lot of fun seeing which of youse can get past Vince and back in without wakin' him."

"Come on," Bill said.

"Ah, all right, you guys talked me into it," Wesley grabbed another doughboy to roast. "Tonight we'll sneak to it. Last one back gets butchered."

Chapter Five

Things especially change in the dark.

The fires were put out and the group walked away. What were once prolific tree branches now seemed like twisted contorted arms ready to grab them. Wesley shivered. He thought of The Raven Hill Butcher when he looked deep enough between the trees and through solid draping darkness. He must've had an odd look on his face, because Wendy asked, "What, did you see something, or…?"

"Huh?"

"You were staring over there between the trees."

"He's thinking of The Butcher already," Bill said.

"I hope he doesn't get you two," Al said.

"I was just thinking about something is all."

"You guys know where the cabin is, right?" Al pointed deep towards the woods on the right. "Over there. Down past the flagpole, just off of the girls' cabins."

"Yeah, yeah, I know where it is."

"Now Wesley, we gotta make this interesting. What's the winner get?"

RETURN TO CAMP SOLGOHACHIA

"Nothing. It's just a competition. Who can get there first then back. Friendly race."

"Well good luck you two," Wendy said, "but I need to get back to my cabin. Uh, bye, Wes. And it was nice meeting you all."

"Bye, Wendy," Wesley said.

Wesley and Wendy looked at each other for a brief second before she left.

She went through the grass and over to the path that led to the girls' cabins. Soon she disappeared into the night.

"You didn't kiss her?" Al asked.

"What? No, we've just met."

"You're smitten," Chester said.

Bill put his arm around Wesley. "Now don't blow this. This cabin thing might impress her."

"How would that impress her?"

"So she knows you're not a wimp."

"I tell you what, Wes," Al said, "if you don't make a move I think I will."

"I seen her first, Al."

"Then go ahead and make a move second."

"I can't make a move this early."

"You see how close she sat next to you dude? She was practically on your lap. She was practically asking for it."

"I don't want to talk about her like this," Wesley said. They came to poor old Panda. "She's a nice girl and I want to take it slow. I was about to tell her we should exchange addresses and numbers, keep in touch after this, until you babbling idiots started to call out to me when we neared the fire."

"Well ya got two weeks," Chester said. "Don't blow it."

Ralph opened the door to the cabin and everybody flooded in, exhausted.

"Where's Vince?" Darren asked.

Everyone ignored his question. They went for their bunks and collapsed.

"I'm exhausted." Wesley kicked off his shoes then threw them off his bunk.

"Now, Wes," Chester said, "girls like ta be treated right. You gotta treat her right."

"I know that. Didn't your mother tell you how I treat her?"

"Hey that's not funny man."

"Relax."

The boys quieted down and most of them changed out of jeans and into shorts. It was nice and cool in the cabin.

Wesley grabbed onto one of the rafters and did a pullup. "Al, Ralph, Chester, you guys ever raced on these things? See who can get to that end and back like monkey bars?"

"That looks dangerous," Ralph said.

"It's harmless. If your arms start to give you can jump to a bunk."

"Jump? And what if I miss? And fall? Split my head open? And down by the door there're no beds."

"Geez, it's like having two Darrens."

"I'll race you," Al said. "It'll be preparation for your race with Bill tonight."

Al climbed the ladder to the top bunk across from Wesley's and grabbed the rafter. He found his balance, then said, "Whenever you're ready."

RETURN TO CAMP SOLGOHACHIA

"Ready," Wesley said. *"Go."*

Wesley pulled himself across the bar, glanced at Al, and saw he was on pace with him.

"When you get to that end you have to smack the wall," Wesley said. "And winner gets Chester's mom."

Chester ran below the race and tried to jump at Wesley's feet but missed.

"Come on Chester we're racing here." Al said. "Knock it off."

Wesley was temporarily distracted and Al took the lead. He kicked into high gear, forgetting to breathe and using all his strength to get to the end as if his life depended on it—but he was too late. Al smacked the wall first.

Wesley focused on getting to the wall and didn't pay attention to what he was hearing behind him—it sounded like an argument was brewing.

Wesley smacked the wall then turned around; Chester was on the beam.

"Really Chester? During the beam race?"

"I'm gonna get you, you faggot."

Chester raced down the beam; his face turned red, he was out of breath—for a skinny guy he wasn't very in shape—and Wesley laughed at him.

Chester came within three feet of Wesley and kicked; Wesley realized his arms were tired but he was still near the door and there was no bed to jump to, just hardwood floors.

"Move it, it's only jokes."

Chester kicked Wesley again so Wesley kicked back.

"Fight! Fight! Fight!" everyone else in the cabin chanted.

NASSER RABADI

Wesley wound his legs back, jumped forward a couple inches, then went for the gut. His foot landed in Chester's stomach; Chester lost his grip momentarily around the beam then regained it. Then he climbed forward as close as he could get to Wesley and tried to hit him with his elbow, then knee him.

At the same time, the door opened and Vince came in confused at the chanting.

"What's with all the yelling and the—" Vince looked up. "Why are you two fighting?"

Wesley said, "Well—"

"I don't wanna hear it. Get down from there immediately."

Chester climbed backwards to the nearby bunk, got off first, then Wesley.

"Now shake hands and apologize. Come on guys, that's a rule. No fighting, and if you do fight, we apologize."

Wesley and Chester sat on the edge of the bunk and shook hands.

"Sorry," Wesley said.

"I'm sorry too."

"Great," Vince said. "I hope that's the end of all our fighting in cabin Panda. I've got zero tolerance for it. Let's all focus on having a great time here. Now it's time for lights out."

Chapter Six

Wesley remembered how things seemed to change in the dark. Hypnotizing coldness slipped through the rusty hinges of the door and through hidden cracks in the structure of the cabin and twisted through his flesh like wire.

He was frightened. He fidgeted with the blue covers he wrapped himself in, and thought how through the haze of gloom and obscurity, they'd soon be racing to that cabin. He had wanted to do it; he had all the confidence in the world this morning when it was daylight. Now in the dark, now after hearing those stories, he was disturbed.

"Wes? You up? Guys?" Bill whispered from the bunk below and startled him.

Wesley turned over, glad Bill couldn't tell how scared he was because the darkness hid everything. "Yeah. Anyone else up?"

"I'm up! I'm up!"

"Shush, you'll wake Vince."

"I'm up too guys," Al said from the bunk across from Wesley. "Ralph? Chester?"

"I'm up."

"Same here."

NASSER RABADI

"Looks like old Vince is knocked out," Al said.

The boys waited in silence for a moment then Wesley climbed down from his bunk. He stood frozen between bunks momentarily, double checking Vince was asleep, then Wesley made his way to the door and looked outside. It was even darker than Wesley had thought. Panic ran through his stomach; he did not feel good about this—but what was a little camp fun? He had never been the one to shy away from such shenanigans.

The others crept over careful not to make noise, careful not to wake Vince, but the floorboards were creaky and they made loud noises.

Thankfully, Vince did not wake up.

The boys all looked out of the windows together, then Wesley went back towards the bunks.

"Chickening out?" Bill whispered.

"Good! Let's not do this! No good can come of this!" Darren said.

"Shut up before ya wake Vince," Chester whispered.

Wesley came back with his flashlight. "You got one too?"

Bill nodded, went to his bag, and pulled out a flashlight.

Al turned the knob slowly; the hinges squealed as he pulled it open a few inches. Al then stopped, turning back to Vince; Vince turned in bed but did not wake up. Al turned his attention back to the door and opened it wider; everybody piled out, then he gently closed it behind them.

"Let's go over the rules," Al said.

"Yeah we definitely should," Bill said. "First one there and back wins. No tripping, hitting, or any other interference."

"How'll we know who actually got there first?" Ralph asked.

RETURN TO CAMP SOLGOHACHIA

"I don't like this one bit!" Darren cried. "You'll die out there! You're crazy for this! The Butcher will get you!"

Al rolled his eyes. "Listen, Darren, it's all made up."

"How about a splinter of wood?" Wesley said. "To prove we actually got there."

"Sounds fair," Bill said. "And if we aren't back in ten minutes then come looking for us."

"Just don't let him getcha guys," Chester said. "I hear he's dying to add new heads to his collection."

Al walked from the door down to the gravel path spanning next to the cabins. "Wes, Bill, come on down here. Get ready, on the count of three…"

Wesley and Bill went down in front of Al, stood in running position, and looked straight ahead. The boys wished each other luck.

"One… *three.*"

The boys were off.

Wesley took the lead with a sudden burst of speed, barefoot feet pounding against grass and soft earth as they went off the gravel path; the night smelled like bark and pine needles. Wind blew hard and knocked his hair into his eyes; Wesley brushed his hair away from his eyes and looked at Bill on his left, who was catching up to him and about to pass him. All at once, Wesley's legs felt stiff. The ground was getting hard and it was hurting to run.

The boys raced across open grass to the center of Camp Solgohachia. The heavy darkness must've shielded them from view of their friends, Wesley thought, and reminded himself to breathe through his nose and not his mouth or else his sides would feel as if they were stabbed with newly sharpened knives.

NASSER RABADI

Wesley and Bill passed the flagpole at the same time; Wesley was losing speed and Bill was ahead of him. Wesley hoped they were going the right direction; he hadn't actually seen the cabin in the four years he had come here, but it was somewhere up ahead in that general area, and he pictured where Charlie had pointed.

His lungs burned for gasps of air; he breathed through his nose as hard as he could and kept pushing. He desperately wanted to win to impress Wendy. His heart pounded so hard he felt it in his throat. Wesley moved his heavy legs with all the strength in his body, feeling chilly air beating against him. All the day's activities had warn him out; he wondered if Bill was as exhausted as he was.

Bill's heavy breathing came from behind Wesley; a smile came across Wesley's face. He was in the lead.

His feet pulsed; *Why had we done this barefoot?* Wesley wondered. They were about to enter the woods.

There was a long stretch of grass before the forest, but soon they'd be stepping over twigs and rocks. Wesley prepared himself for the pain of the hidden forest floor and for the intensity of the run back. And the flashlight wouldn't do him much good—he couldn't figure out what was on the ground in the brief seconds they were illuminated while he ran furiously.

He and Bill weaved past remains of fires from earlier, and the ground was littered with green sticks and remnants of doughboys and smores and sunflower seeds that were in the process of being devoured by ants and flies. Wesley shivered, remembering the time he saw a whole ocean of ants in the neighbor's front yard when the neighbors were turning up the ground to put in new soil. The way they moved like static on a television screen made him sick; the

RETURN TO CAMP SOLGOHACHIA

way they moved, even in chaos, Wesley wondered if they were all connected as one big mind. But what had developed his biggest fear of bugs—even worse than the bee sting on his foot—was the time he heard about a baby who was found getting eaten alive by ants.

But now wasn't the time to think about that; the woods were an arm's length away, and Bill was a step ahead of him.

As they came into the woods, Wesley took the lead. The race was neck and neck; back and forth. It would be a tight one.

Fifteen feet into the woods, the boys came upon the cabin. Jagged and faulty, as if constructed by blind men. Splintery planks were sprawled across the windows and doors with rusty nails, nails that seemed they'd turn to dust if touched. It was nothing more than a ghostly silhouette—it shuddered in the wind, creaking in the night, home to clusters of spiders. Dust lay over the cabin like a layer of dirty snow. Nasty weeds twisted up from the ground and worked their way upon the sides of the cabin as if attracted like magnets.

Wesley and Bill looked at each other; the boys had come to a halt.

"Woah." Wesley whispered, then ran the final five feet to its front door.

"Dang it." Bill bolted after him.

Wesley fastened his hands around a loose section of wood at the very end—a splinter that was almost falling off around the nail, as if it had been crafted and waiting there for Wesley Lawrence to come and pick it off.

He ripped it free then looked at Bill, who even through the veil of night looked pale. His hand was frozen on the plank across the broken glass of the front window; his eyes stared holes through Wesley.

"Bill? Are you okay?"

Bill stared silently.

"Out with it. What's going on?"

Wesley was paralyzed; scared to look behind him—was there someone there? Was that what Bill was afraid of?

A gust of cold wind swept through the trees and Wesley jumped.

"Wesley," Bill said strangely, "is that a snake?"

Wesley followed Bill's eyes down at the small three- or four-foot space between each other. There, creeping along the ground up the front wall of the building, was a snake at least four feet long—probably longer.

Together they screamed.

Wesley clutched the splinter so hard it was buried in his palm and probably left smaller splinters in his skin.

Wesley took off; behind him he heard Bill still screaming. When he turned around, he saw Bill had fallen, and the snake was staring at him with its head upside down from the wall of the cabin.

"Dang it Bill."

"Ohmigod."

Wesley turned back and helped Bill up; the snake writhed down. Both of them screamed—yelling at the top of their lungs as it came off the cabin walls and flowed to the grass and after them.

The boys backed away from the woods, not daring to take their eyes off the serpent, but soon lost track of it while it slithered through tall grass and vanished. It could have been anywhere.

"Where'd it go?" Bill asked.

"I'll be damned if I know."

"No, we'll be damned if we don't know."

RETURN TO CAMP SOLGOHACHIA

Together they inched backwards, gasping, and Wesley figured they'd walk slowly backwards until they came back to Panda. Now that would be a sight. He already imagined the guys laughing at them. Wendy would probably laugh too if she were there… Wesley turned red thinking about it.

But after a minute more of walking backwards the boys turned around and screamed again when they ran into their friends. Al, Darren, Ralph, and Chester.

"Fellas, what's the matter with you?" Al asked.

"Was there… was there ghosts?" Darren asked. "It's The Raven Hill Butcher isn't it!"

"I want to go home," Ralph cried.

Chester was the only one laughing. "What a couple of pansies."

Then, in the distance, footfalls.

Chester squealed. "Who's there?"

Al hit him on the shoulder. "Quiet, moron."

A shape emerged from the darkness; the boys stared at it.

As it came closer, it took form and they saw it was Wendy.

"Are you guys okay?" she asked. "I heard screaming."

"Wendy?" Wesley said. "What are you doing here?"

Wendy came closer before answering. "I couldn't sleep and was thinking about your race. I was coming by to see if you guys were awake when I heard screaming. Did you see something?"

"There was a big snake."

"About four feet long—maybe more, maybe five," Bill said. "I couldn't even grab my splinter of wood."

"Oh yeah." Wesley held up his splinter nice and high. "Guess that means I won."

"I guess it does." Al yawned. "I'm tired."

"Let's get going," Wesley said. "I don't wanna stick around for that thing to come back."

"Hey," Wendy said, "at least it wasn't The Butcher."

Things *do* especially change in the dark—more so than any of the kids knew.

Something had been awakened—something brewed underground, deep within the earth. The ground of the woods trembled; leaves drifted from the dirt next to the old cabin as if trying to run away. Chilling winds drilled past the grass and sank into the dirt. The crescent moon shone its light down on the cabin and winked off the broken remnants of what had once been windows.

The ground shook abruptly, and its loose soil opened.

One filthy black hand broke the surface of the earth and clawed. It dug its other hand free and dredged away handfuls of dirt until its decaying head was pulled through.

It dragged itself out of its tomb, coming up from one black abyss to another, and listened to the laughter of children—the children who awoke him.

He stepped forward—it was more a wobble than a walk. He'd have to get used to walking again now that he had escaped his crypt. From far away he watched; six boys in one direction, and a young lady in another.

It was hard to smile, but his sore muscles found a way.

RETURN TO CAMP SOLGOHACHIA

After the kids disappeared, he turned back to the cabin he had once lived in and broke the board off the door; it was easy to remove. Rusty nails crumbled and he tossed the wood towards the swaying trees.

Inside the cabin it was as black as a cat but he didn't need to see; he remembered how it looked in the light and he knew where he had hidden it.

At his right, he found the bathroom, and felt along the wall behind the rotting old door for the loose panel of wood. It fell to the ground as soon as he touched it.

Sure enough, it was where he had left it all those years ago.

His knife had done so much damage; the long blade set in aging wood felt so natural in his hands, as if they hadn't been apart a day.

He was only missing his mask.

"Look at you," Darren said, "you've got her!"

"Calm down Darren, she only came by 'cause she heard screaming, it don't mean a thing."

"You've gotta be blind I tell ya," Chester said. "Why do you keep denying it?"

"Blind as a bat," Bill said.

The boys approached the cabin, surprised that only Wendy and nobody else had come towards the screaming. But maybe nobody else heard. Maybe.

Wesley yawned. "You think we woke up Vince?"

"No," Bill said. "He would have woken up the whole camp by now looking for us. He's a hardass."

Al opened the door slowly; it squeaked. Inside, the boys found Vince snoring very loudly. The floor creaked under their footsteps, but they found their ways back into their beds without waking Vince—he must've been a heavy sleeper, and Wesley thought about inventing a game where they could see who could make the most noise without waking him up. He thought how funny it would be to light a firecracker and see Vince waking up from the sounds thinking they were gunshots.

Wesley curled the covers over himself; yawned then shut his eyes. He kept the wood from the abandoned cabin on the windowsill next to his bunk.

Minutes later he heard snoring but Wesley himself couldn't sleep yet. He just wasn't tired anymore after all the screaming and the sudden boost of adrenaline. He laid there thinking, replaying the fun day of camp in his mind. He was actually glad he came to camp.

Somewhere along the replay, dreamless sleep found him.

Chapter Seven

"Rise and shine campers!"

It was first thing in the morning and Vince was already speaking at the top of his lungs, waking everybody up. There were a few groans, some of the guys were turning back over to sleep, but Vince kept on marching around the cabin nearly yelling.

"Good morning fellas, good morning. Up, up, up, come on guys. Ralphie, wake on up. You up there—Wesley—come on, wake up."

Wesley rubbed his eyes, looked around, and saw Chester sliding out of bed, and Bill and Darren and Al already fixing their sheets with glazed over eyes. He and Ralph were the last two awake.

He yawned, shut his eyes for a moment and sat up a little, then almost fell asleep again while sitting up.

"Up, up, up, Mr. Wesley. Time for breakfast then to get the day started!"

Leave me alone, Wesley thought.

He groaned, slipped out from the covers, then fixed his bed. Then he climbed down the ladder and went to the bathroom to relieve himself then brush his teeth. After that, when he came back to change into a new shirt and pants and to throw on his shoes, most of the cabin had left besides Bill and Darren who decided to stay behind to wait for him.

"What's the point of a counselor?" Wesley sat on Bill's bunk to slide his socks on. "Is he just here to be our personal alarm clock? Dude doesn't even know when six kids sneak out of the cabin at night."

"I think so," Bill said. "Vince is annoying for sure but it's his job."

When Bill was ready the boys left Panda and headed for the cafeteria. The line was short—most kids were already served.

"Hold up," Darren said. "Oh man, I left my retainer case in the cabin. I'll be right back you guys."

"Suit yourself," Wesley said.

Darren sprinted away.

"Fastest I've ever seen him run, Bill."

"He doesn't know he could wrap it in napkins, does he?"

"Probably scared he might throw them out by accident again."

The wait in line was six or seven minutes, then they were served little cartons of milk, single serve plastic containers of cereal, and their choice of either an apple, pear, or banana.

Wesley and Bill sat by one of the windows; they didn't see their cabinmates or Wendy anywhere. Wesley tried to look through the window up the path to Panda but it was a little too obscure at his angle in the back of the cafeteria and he could only see the first half of the path.

"You see Darren anywhere? What's taking him?" Wesley asked. It had been about ten minutes since Darren left.

"No clue—fatty might've had a heart attack on the way there or back. Might've ran out of breath. Might take him a year to catch it."

RETURN TO CAMP SOLGOHACHIA

Wesley laughed. "Yeah, maybe. He runs out of breath lifting a spoon to his mouth."

"As soon as we get back, we're putting him on a diet. No chocolate no sugar no nothing. No ifs ands or buts about it."

"We'll make him walk a mile a day."

"Let's start small. Half a mile a day."

"Nah dude, he can walk a mile. I think."

"Three or four laps around the block, Wes?"

"We'll just put him on the treadmill, doesn't his family have a treadmill in the basement?"

"Yeah—yeah I think they do. And I don't think any of them have ever used it."

"How's he not use it every night then?"

"Beats me." Bill shrugged.

Wesley yawned. "No sign of the others, huh?"

Bill looked around with him. "Nope. You see Wendy?"

"Nope."

"What's on the agenda for today?"

"Think they're gonna put us into teams, after breakfast. They'll probably start the competitions soon. I think I'm gonna ditch 'em all this year."

Bill shrugged. "Don't do that. Have some fun. It's our last year here."

"I wanna ditch and get alone with Wendy. Or maybe we can ditch and pull some pranks. Let's find Darren soon and talk about it. Let's all try and get on the same team again."

NASSER RABADI

Darren huffed on his walk back to Panda. It was a hot cloudless day and that made it worse; sweat dripped into his eyes and burned. He stopped, leaned against a tree, and rubbed his eyes. A moment later he continued up the slope to the cabins; it was a pain walking uphill. After three steps up he was out of breath.

The inside of Panda was refreshingly cool. Darren sat on the edge of his bed and found his retainer case on the windowsill. He laid down to catch his breath.

"God I'm out of shape," Darren said. Then when he was ready to rejoin Bill and Wesley, he left his bed and went across the cabin. "When I get home, no more Twinkies. Or Jolt Cola. Or Tootsie Rolls. Or…"

Darren was blinded by the sheet that was wrapped around his face and choked him; powerful arms pulled him against his attacker's body. Darren strained to hit the menace away but he couldn't move; he was paralyzed under the monster's grip.

He had never been more scared in his life.

His struggle to breathe worsened when the rope was set around his throat. It pulled tighter by the second. Suddenly he knew that this was it. He was going to die.

After Wesley and Bill finished eating, they still hadn't seen Darren, so they walked back to Panda. Along the way they kept an eye out for Vince, Al, Chester, or Ralph—maybe one of them had seen Darren, or maybe he was hanging out with them—but the boys didn't see any of their bunkmates.

"Not like him to miss breakfast," Wesley said halfway through the gravel path.

"I thought he'd only be a minute," Bill said. "We better not walk in on him jerking off."

Wesley laughed. "Yeah, wouldn't be the first time."

"That's fucking gross."

Wesley opened the door then walked in first; Bill followed closely.

"Darren?" Bill called out, then they were both chilled and suspended in place.

However badly they had screamed last night, their screams after walking into Panda were worse. Wesley's throat strained; he couldn't believe it. He couldn't believe—his eyes darted away, darted back; he was too disturbed to keep looking at it, but his eyes rolled back to Darren.

He ran.

The rope weas tense and strained under Darren's massive weight.

"Darren ohmigod ohmigod what the hell what the—"

A thin sheet was fastened over his head under the noose and covered part of his body; they couldn't see his face but they knew it was him.

Wesley and Bill climbed up the nearest bunkbed and reached to bring him down. Bill wrapped his arms around Darren's torso, attempted to lift him to try and stop any choking. Wesley loosened the rope from the rafters and helped Bill to bring him down to the bed.

NASSER RABADI

Darren's body was slack—loose and malleable under their grips. Almost rubbery. Almost as if it weren't a real person.

Wesley struggled to rip the sheet and the noose off of him—after a minute of struggles it slipped right off, without a single movement from the boy underneath them.

"Darren? My God Darren—"

His eyes were sunken, his skin was turning purple and waxy. His neck was snapped.

"He's dead he's dead!" Bill screamed. *"Why would he do that?"*

Wesley jumped off the bed, fell on his knees on the floor and heaved. His stomach clenched. Heat ran through him; everything was blurry. *"He didn't do it. He couldn't."*

"The hell do you mean he couldn't, Wes? Do you—do you see him? He did it."

"How's a lard like Darren gonna pull himself onto the rafters? He's never been able to climb—"

"I don't know Wes! But he's dead, look at him."

"Ohmigod Bill, he can't be dead. He was fine on the way to break-fast."

"If he didn't… what—what does this mean?"

"The Butcher." it was the first thing to come to Wesley's mind. *"Don't you think for one minute there was some truth to those legends?"*

Bill came down from the top bunk and joined Wesley on the floor. Bill sat with his legs crossed, wiping away tears. He opened his mouth to speak then shut it.

Wesley gulped. "You remember what Al said about The Butcher?"

"Is now the time for a story?"

RETURN TO CAMP SOLGOHACHIA

Wesley went on anyways. "I've… I've… oh God, forgive me, Bill. This is all my fault."

"Your fault?"

"Fear brings The Butcher to life and I'm *scared.* What if I woke him? What if *we all* woke him?"

Bill didn't say anything.

Wesley cried. *"What if we woke him?"*

Chapter Eight

C harlie the camp director held a camp-wide meeting to discuss the situation, but Wesley could hardly pay attention.

"We have some awful news. Some terrible news—"

He didn't kill himself.

"—found dead—"

We woke him.

"Camp will proceed as normal, however—"

If we hadn't done the stupid race if we hadn't gone to the cabin he'd still be alive I just know it. I don't know how I can prove it, but I know it. I know there's some truth to the legends. There has to be. It all had to stem from something. There are things we can't explain in this world, Wesley, you know that. The Butcher may be one of those things…

"—always talk to someone—"

Wesley was angry hearing Charlie talk about Darren as if he knew what he was talking about. *Always talk to someone. Darren didn't need someone to talk to—he was murdered. And… and all of us were there. Me. Bill. Darren. Al. Chester. Ralph.* Wendy. *One down, six to go.*

"If any of you have any questions—"

RETURN TO CAMP SOLGOHACHIA

How do we stop this thing? How do we stop The Raven Hill Butcher? I know—I just know—it was him. Someone had to do it. It wasn't Darren. He could hardly lift a ten-pound barbell, there was no way he lifted himself up to the rafter.

Vince talked to the boys from Panda after the camp-wide meeting in a cabin-wide meeting. The boys all sat on their bunks and Vince stood in front of them, but Wesley zoned out during this meeting as well. He wasn't sure how much he could take of it. Stories about The Raven Hill Butcher flooded his mind. He wanted to yell at Vince to shut up but held his tongue; he felt his cheeks growing hot with blood, and everything in front of him was a blur. All he could think about was the touch of Darren's dead body—he wondered what happened to it now, if it were on its way back to town, how they broke the news to Darren's parents. Wesley wondered if the news had spread to his family yet. He planned to call them eventually—but for now he was too stunned to talk to them or anyone.

I will kill him—I will kill whoever did this to you. I will kill him myself. That's a promise, buddy. I'll kill him I'll kill him.

After the meeting, the scheduled activities were starting—Wesley guessed they missed getting their wristbands that indicated what team they'd be on for the duration of camp, since they were here in the cabin—but the boys from Panda ditched anyways, and gathered in the woods behind their cabin and sat down to have a real meeting about Darren for once—the previous two were utter bull crap.

NASSER RABADI

Wesley stood before his friends. "Darren didn't do it. Outside of me 'n Bill, you guys didn't know him, but I think you understand he—he couldn't have killed himself like the counselors think. He couldn't have lifted himself up there to that rafter—he wasn't strong enough to hang himself."

"This is screwed up," Al said.

Bill ran his hands over his face speechlessly.

"We need to stick together," Wesley said. Then, after a pause, added: "It was The Butcher."

"He ain't real," Chester said. "Have ya lost your mind?"

"Listen to me for one minute, don't you remember what Al said? That's his cabin. That's why people said they've seen him in this camp, that's why he's killed people who weren't far from here. If it's his cabin, if we disturbed it, if we brought him back—"

"Listen, Wes," Al said, "I know this is a seriously tough time, isn't it? But think straight for a minute, okay? If we brought him back now, how did he kill those girls a few years ago?"

"Then maybe it was someone else or maybe he was already back. I don't have all the answers. And maybe he saw us last night. Maybe he's coming for us all who were there. Darren, you, me, all of us, and Wendy."

"Then why's he come for Darren first?"

"He was the most sacred, and he was alone."

RETURN TO CAMP SOLGOHACHIA

Activities between battling camp teams—Apache, Navajo, Cherokee, Shawnee, depending on which color wristband you pulled from a bucket—were scattered throughout the day, leaving campers with a lot of free time to do whatever they want. Some went canoeing, some were playing basketball, some were playing carpetball, some sat around and walked, but as for Wesley, he slumped in his hiding spot beneath the deck of the cafeteria.

He needed to be alone. Bill had believed him, but just barely. The others not at all—although he suspected Ralph was scared enough that he might have had a little belief in it. Right now he didn't even know where Bill was—last he saw him, Bill was trying to play golf. He almost hated Bill for trying to move on so quickly, but what was Bill supposed to do? Maybe Bill was just trying to take his mind off of…

So Wesley hid in darkness, twisting a twig between his fingers, wiping away sweat with the collar of his white t-shirt, feeling small beams of hot sun sneak through cracks and warm his body.

He wanted to leave. There'd be no leaving for about twelve more days. The road wasn't very far from camp. And he knew a shortcut. If he had to go back through the entrance near the parking lot, it would take at least two hours on foot to reach the main road. But going through the woods, he could reach the road in ten minutes. He learned of the shortcut his first year when exploring with Bill and Darren and still remembered where in the woods it was and how to get there.

His stomach clenched.

He listened to the sounds of the golfers afar off and tried to process how this could be real or why the camp would still be going. It was sick to him that camp was still happening.

Footsteps came from his left. He snapped the twig in half; he figured he knew who it was.

"Wesley?"

Then a few seconds later, she came into view.

"Yeah."

"Is there, uh, space for me in there?"

Wesley didn't say anything; she crawled under there with him. They sat silently for a moment until Wendy said, "Sorry. I'm so sorry."

Wesley wanted to say thanks but said nothing instead.

"I ran into some of your friends, they're all worried about you. They didn't know where you were, but I told them I knew where I'd find you."

"Down here makes for a pretty good place to be alone."

"Should I go?"

"No, I like having you here."

"Is it fine if I ask you what happened?"

Wesley brushed his tears away, embarrassed to cry in front of her, but at the same time also not caring that she saw his tears. "The others wouldn't listen to me, Wendy. I need you to listen to me. I really need you to. Because unless we do something… he's coming for us too."

"What do you mean?"

"It's true. I don't know which parts are true but fear brough The Raven Hill Butcher back, that's what happened last night at our race. Darren didn't hang himself. He was too fat to reach the rafters and to do all of that… he'd never have succeeded. What we did last night awoke The Butcher. All seven of us who were there… he's coming to get us now Wendy. Starting with Darren maybe because he was most scared or because he was alone."

Wendy was silent.

"You're on his list. I am, Bill is, Al, Ralph, Chester. Any of us can be next."

"Wes…"

"Yeah?"

She gulped. "You really believe he's out there, don't you?"

"I do. I don't know how I do or why I do—but I do. I can feel it. Something wrong is going on here. Something seriously wrong."

Wesley spent most of day two at Camp Solgohachia hiding, and Wendy joined him for some of it. They talked about everything in the world, they talked about her life in Radley before Raven Hill, they talked about their dreams and their fears.

They exchanged addressed—at least briefly during the horrors, he was able to smile—and they discovered they weren't very far from each other at all. Wesley tried to talk to her about videogames but she wasn't very much interested in that—although she had entertained the idea of going to the arcade with him back home.

If we survive, Wesley thought.

He had a little doubt about The Raven Hill Butcher. There was no trace of him, but it only made sense that it was him. Wesley had debated this with himself heavily throughout the day until that night when he went to bed, forgetting about his rule to not lay directly on the old musty mattress and laying his body against it.

He had always believed in an afterlife because that was the thing to do—everyone he knew believed in one, but did he only believe in one because others did, or did he truly feel there was one? And where did Darren go in the afterlife if it did in fact exist?

There's no way to separate fact from fiction, not with The Butcher. Too many things that I'm not sure about. Like Al said, if he killed those girls, how did we awaken him now? He was already awake, unless someone else put him to sleep between then and now and we just undid it all. Or unless… a killer was still on the loose and he wasn't the real *Butcher, the man who killed the girls. And we may have just summoned the real deal.*

We have no idea what we're dealing with here. It could be anything. Somebody's hurt Darren and somebody wants to hurt me and my friends. Be careful.

He shut his eyes. Soon he was asleep and his mind was filled with dreams of being back home, being at peace, playing videogames with Bill and Darren, and then going down to the gas station for a soda before hitting the arcade. The way things used to be; the way things should still be. But things would never be the same again.

Chapter Nine

Morning brought fresh sunlight and a new sense of hope, although it was a drag to look down and see Darren's bunk empty. But there was nothing Wesley could do. Darren was gone and that was it. It was impossible to process. Tears started to come but he wiped them away.

Vince was going over the usual spiel in the morning, and he might've said something about Darren and asked how they boys were holding up, but Wesley zoned him out again. His head hurt and he wondered what day three had in store—hopefully no more terror. He had enough terror for one lifetime. The image of the broken bones in Darren's neck poking against skin and threatening to escape would haunt him forever. He wondered if he could ever forget it.

The morning had him wondering *Why* as he got ready. If it hadn't been murder, then why just why would he do it then? Early in the morning. Forgetting his retainer. Did he just… walk back to the cabin and think, *You know what Darren this must be a great time to kill yourself. Nice and early in the morning. Everybody's at breakfast. Why don't we just climb on up here, tie a noose—let's just pull that from thin air—tie it up, put a sheet around your head, then the noose, and let's kill myself. Sounds good Darren. Note? Nah, note not included—note not necessary. The guys don't need to know why.*

No scenario made sense.

Wesley fixed his bunk then dressed in the first shorts and t-shirt he could find. He noticed after putting on his shoes that Vince was standing by the door although he was ready. He was waiting for all the boys to finish so he could watch them leave. Maybe he had covered that in one of his speeches, maybe he hadn't. Wesley didn't know one way or the other—he didn't pay attention to a word from the adults. It was hard to focus.

And when he and the rest of Panda left the cabin at the same time, he had a very bad feeling that something terrible was about to happen.

Wesley and Bill stuck together; the others went their own way. They sat on one of the metal benches next to the basketball courts, sun beating on them heavily, and Wesley launched pebbles at unsuspecting passersby.

Normally he'd have fun with that, but after a few minutes and hitting two campers, he gave up. He put the slingshot at his side, stared off into camp, watched people move in a blur. Watched people move happily, watched people going from place to place with friends, watched people play games.

RETURN TO CAMP SOLGOHACHIA

None of them cared about Darren; it was as if he had never died. None of them cared. All of them went on with life. Was that what was gonna happen after Wesley died? Was everybody going to be happy and live their life as if he were still there, or had never existed at all?

None of them knew Darren, he understood that. But none of them showed any sadness—how could that be?

Wesley frowned and turned to Bill; Bill was looking at his feet.

"I can't make heads or tails of it. I can't wrap my mind around it."

"I don't think we ever will." Bill wiped sweat away with his shirt collar. "Don't make it any easier that we're stuck here supposed to be having fun."

"Look at them, all happy. Should they be so happy?"

"They didn't know him. Forgive them."

Wesley didn't know what to say.

"Poor Darren."

"Yeah, poor Darren." Wesley grabbed a pebble and fidgeted with it. "I want to go home."

"Yeah. Me too."

"We never should have raced."

"But we didn't know."

"We still never should have done it. We never should have—"

"It's not your fault, Wesley. Please don't try and convince yourself that it is, it isn't."

It was probably twenty minutes later when they heard the first scream; it was followed by a second, much louder one, then it became a sea of screams—everybody froze. Wesley looked around but couldn't tell what he was supposed to be seeing—the screams were coming from far away but everything was still. Even the screams quieted down for a moment, but that didn't last long. Soon campers were running away from the left end of the camp and towards the far right where Wesley and Bill were.

Counselors ran around telling kids to calm down.

Wesley turned to Bill. "You don't think…"

Bill was pale. "I hope not."

"Oh God, who did he…"

Wesley stood up; it was so silent now he could've heard a blade of grass grow. He noticed some kids look at him then look away. Wesley rushed off the bench, and Bill followed. The two pushed past clusters of people while counselors yelled at them to stay put, but they didn't listen—they sprinted toward the small crowd around the flagpole, and the counselors didn't stop them.

At the head of the crowd were Al and Ralph; Al ran his hands through his hair angrily, and Ralph cried uncontrollably and tried to mutter something incoherent. There were other campers—all girls—crying as they attempted to explain something to some counselors. They must've been the ones who discovered the body.

The body was nearly impossible to find through the crowd of kids and the counselors trying to shield the body away from curious observers, but Wesley saw a wrist on the ground, slashed open half an inch deep and nearly severing it totally from its arm.

Wesley grabbed his stomach then looked away. *"Oh hell."*

Bill stared blankly at it; Wesley helped him turn away. Al and Ralph moved closer to them.

"He got him," Al whispered. "He got him. He got Chester."

RETURN TO CAMP SOLGOHACHIA

It was ruled suicide.

There was a second camp-wide meeting. Al, Ralph, Wesley, Bill, and Wendy sat together in the back. This time it wasn't at the flagpole but in the cafeteria. Everybody was seated, and camp director Charlie paced up and down the middle aisle.

Al had told Wesley what happened: some girls stumbled upon Chester's body at the flagpole. Al and Ralph thought Chester had gone to play baseball and they hadn't seen him for a while—but there he was. Dead. *Both* wrists slit so deep they weren't sure how he could physically do that with the knife they found near the trail to the cabins.

Why kill slit his wrists then run to the flagpole?

Wesley didn't believe Chester had done it at all. He knew it had to be The Raven Hill Butcher—and Al and Ralph and Wendy finally believed Wesley and Bill. Wesley couldn't say he was happy about the circumstances.

He trembled; he worried who would be next. And he could only think of one way to escape it: to run away. To find a way back home. It would be dangerous and would take hours but it was the only way out of this madhouse.

Wesley thought, *I'll give Mom and Dad a call. And if they can't bring me home I'm leaving. The Butcher might find his way out of the camp but he doesn't know where I live, he can't just find me. I'll be long gone from here.*

Why did we have to disturb his cabin? Why? Just why?

NASSER RABADI

Charlie and Vince were in the private counselors-only room on the other side of the cafeteria building where campers were never allowed to enter. Vince pulled on the collar of his purple Camp Solgohachia shirt that all the counselors had to wear. It was burning in here.

"Vince, this is the second kid from your cabin…"

Vince nervously tapped his fingers on the table. "I'm aware."

"Parents are going to ask questions. We're going to be ruined. Is there anything you can think of—anything that might clue us in on why these boys have done this? Some sort of pact? Some sort of… some sort of—"

"Pact? What do you think this is?"

"Two kids from the same cabin don't kill themselves for no reason."

Vince nodded, then tapped his fingers more frequently on the table. "You saw that kid's wrists, Charlie. They were too deep—he didn't do that on his own. And I don't think the other kid hung himself either."

"Did any of the kids fight with each other? Did any of them not get along?"

"This boy that… slit his wrists, Chester, um, he had a problem with another boy named Wesley."

"Wesley? Which one is he?"

"Wesley wouldn't do that, I'm sure."

"Are you absolutely sure, Vincent?"

"I think so."

"You think or you know?"

Vince paused. "I will watch him. I'll keep a close eye on him."

RETURN TO CAMP SOLGOHACHIA

"Yes or no. Do you know if Wesley—if Wesley was mad enough to do this?"

"I don't know, okay? I don't know."

Charlie kicked the wall; his shoe left a black mark behind. "This could ruin us. Come on, it's time to address the kids."

Wesley bit his nails; it seemed to him Vince and Charlie were looking directly at him—but that couldn't be right, could it? Had they seen him and Bill that night racing? Had Vince been awake that whole time? Did they know about The Raven Hill Butcher? Did they think it was Wesley's fault? He had been the only one to bring back a souvenir…

What if that souvenir was the whole reason any of this happened?

Wesley thought of the snake and tearing off the wood—how scared they had been. It almost made sense that The Butcher would go after the most frightened first, being Darren, but Chester? More terrified than Ralph? Maybe Chester had done a good job at hiding it.

Are two deaths enough? Will they finally call off camp? I can't wait to get out of here…

Wesley didn't realize Charlie had already begun his speech. "We've had another unfortunate… accident—"

Wesley's hands formed into fists. *Accident?*

He thought it was bullshit how Charlie was acting—as if this were normal. As if this were standard procedure. In all four of Wesley's years here, the most he had seen was a sprained ankle or a broken pinky finger, and that was rare. This was two murders in a row. Why wouldn't Charlie just say what it was and send them all home? Did they want this to continue? Wesley was confused.

"Please," Charlie said a few minutes later when Wesley started paying attention again, "if any of you are remotely thinking about it, don't do it. There's help. There's always someone here to help you. Find an adult—any of our counselors or staff or even myself. Please. Things get better."

No matter what Charlie said, Wesley knew it was endless hills of bullshit.

After it was over, Wesley felt sick. After the camp-wide meeting, he went to the bathroom then washed his hands. Strangely, after he left the bathroom, he noticed Vince eyeing him, and noticed that as he went towards the door to leave the cafeteria, Vince stood up and followed him out, trying to trail a few feet away and remain hidden, but he could feel him watching.

Wesley didn't say a word to him—he just kept on going through the camp. Wesley wondered why Vince was following him, and how long was he going to do it for? What did he want? What did he think he was gonna find?

So instead of going straight for the phone like he had planned, he circled back around the flagpole—the blood wasn't all cleaned yet off of it—then went from there through camp and back to the cafeteria to use the water fountain on the inside. Still, he noticed, Vince following him discretely. Except he didn't follow him into the cafeteria this time, he waited around the outside for Wesley to come back. At least he was *trying* to be sneaky, but not succeeding.

RETURN TO CAMP SOLGOHACHIA

Wesley left from another exit. He went to the little giftshop building that sold Camp Solgohachia shirts and baseball caps as well as candy bars and flashlights and sun screen, and went to the back of the shop where there was a payphone and little bit of privacy. He searched his pockets for change, put a quarter through the slot, then dialed home.

It rang for a while, and he worried for a minute that they wouldn't answer—maybe they were out getting ice cream or walking the dog—but after a long while, Mom did pick up the phone.

"Hello?"

"Mom, it's me, I'm calling from camp. I really need you to pick me up."

"Pick you up? Is it… oh honey, this is about Darren, isn't it? I am so sorry honey."

"Well yes Mom, but another kid… did something similar and I want to go home."

"Another? Oh my…"

"So can you come and get me?"

"I'm afraid I can't do that, your father needs the car for work. I can't just borrow it for *such* a long trip. I'm sorry about Darren honey. And sorry about the other kid. I hope you understand."

"But Mom—"

"I'm sorry, but I can't drop everything we're doing to pick you up. It's only a few more days."

"Mom, two kids are dead."

"I'm sorry Wesley. Be careful, okay? We'll be seeing you soon. You always have a good time at camp. Just stick close to Bill and make some new friends."

73

NASSER RABADI

"I am sticking close to Bill and I have made new friends, Mom, damnit, but I need to leave. You don't underst—"

"Don't use that language with me young man. I'll make you wash your mouth with soap."

"Goodbye Mom. I love you."

"Goodbye honey. See you soon. I'm sorry about Darren."

He hung up the phone aware that it could have been the last time he ever talked to his mother.

It was hot out and he couldn't find Bill again and he felt sick, so he went back to the cabin to lay down for a little bit. Wesley went through the path and passed the other cabins, jealous knowing that all their friends were alive.

Wesley felt cursed. The Raven Hill Butcher was coming for everybody who was at the cabin that night. Would he be next?

He went into Panda and shut the door. He stood for a moment under the spot where they had found Darren. Wesley wept. "I'm so sorry Darren. I'm so sorry."

Then he went to the back and washed his face in one of the sinks when the door to Panda opened. Wesley called out, "Hello? Who's there?"

There was no answer, only fast footfalls coming through the cabin towards him. Wesley looked up from the sink, and Vince turned the corner.

"Why are you following me? What is this?"

RETURN TO CAMP SOLGOHACHIA

Vince raised a fist. "Thought you could ditch me? Why so eager to get away? *Boy.* I know you had a problem with Chester. You tell me now if you had anything to do with it."

Wesley stared at him.

Vince grabbed Wesley by the collar and pulled him closer. "You tell me right this minute. You know he couldn't have slit both his wrists that deep—I know it, the camp knows it, so if you did something I swear to God—"

"You're freaking crazy man. You're sick. I wouldn't do that—I couldn't. I was watching basketball when he—when someone—when it happened. You maniac. Vince you're a psycho."

Vince threw him to the floor.

"Screw you. Maybe I did do it. then I'm the last person you should be fucking with. I'll gut you like a fish."

"You're screwed up in the head." Vince turned around and left.

Wesley looked at the floor until he heard the door slam shut. His hands were in fists. He couldn't believe a counselor had just put his hands on him and accused him of murder. He was not a murderer, but if he suddenly decided to become one, Vince would be where he would start.

Vince left the cabin and thought, *Charlie's right, it's him.*

Two black gloved hands came around the corner of the cabin and pressed so tightly to his throat that not even his squeals could escape. Vince was pulled behind Panda into the woods; the person dragged him far until the cabins were just a memory.

The figure pushed Vince into a tree and held him with one hand by a throat. Vince tried to scream but it was locked inside of him; he looked into the eyes of madman behind a black mask. His attacker wore a filthy groundskeeper outfit.

The man lifted his blade set in aging wood; in that moment Vince remembered all the stories—but he couldn't reminisce about them for long.

The Raven Hill Butcher brought the knife halfway through Vince's skull and watched him squirm and writhe. Vince's eyes twitched, pleaded, begged; they fluttered shut then creaked open again, and his body convulsed. The Butcher removed the blade—Vince wiggled like a torn worm—then sank it into Vince's pelvis and dragged it downward.

Blood leaked out of the counselor; The Butcher used him as practice. He raised the blade up above his head and slammed it into Vince's shoulder. His arm came off in one clean swoop. If anybody found Vince, he would be unrecognizable and split into chunks scattered throughout the camp woods.

Chapter Ten

Night fell upon Camp Solgohachia and with it came the bonfires again—awful doughboys and stale smores passed around and creepy   tales
e   x   -
changed.

Tonight was not a normal night. The moon was full and its light came brightly upon the camp. Wesley didn't feel like eating any doughboys or anything tonight—his stomach couldn't take it. He was too nervous for what he was about to do.

To his left was Wendy, to his right was Al, and across from him were Bill and Ralph.

And then there were five.

"I can't believe a counselor would do that to you," Wendy said. "We've got to tell someone. Charlie, or—"

"No, it doesn't matter. It wouldn't matter at all. I don't know if any of you phoned home. Well, I did. Nobody can come pick me up, so I'm leaving. The four of you are welcome to join. Seven's already become five. I can't stick around to see it become four, then three, then two, then one, then zero. We're all bound to die if we stay. The adults are useless, they can't help us."

"I'm in," Bill said.

The others agreed too.

"We'll all go tonight. What time is it?"

Al looked at his watch. "Nearing nine."

"Light's out is ten. Eleven on the dot, let's all meet over there." Wes pointed down towards trees on the far end of camp, somewhere after the boys' cabins. "One year I went exploring there and found a shortcut to a road. Bill you were there, you might remember. You me and Darren."

"I do."

"I didn't… I didn't think this was what I was getting into with Raven Hill," Wendy said. "When we moved here—"

"It's Raven Hill," Wesley said. "What did you expect?"

In panda, the boys packed their bags. Wesley slipped the woodchip in his pocket then asked, "Anyone seen Vince?"

Nobody had.

"Maybe you really did kill him," Ralph said nervously. "You didn't kill him did you?"

Wesley laughed—it felt strange to laugh in a time like this, strange but good. "No I didn't. Nothing to worry about Ralph."

"I've got a knife, anyone else have one?" Al asked.

He was the only one.

After they were done, Wesley turned on his flashlight, and the boys left the dark cabin and set out into the night. It was ten-fifty.

RETURN TO CAMP SOLGOHACHIA

Wesley figured Wendy would be heading out now too unless she fell asleep or chickened out. Wesley and the boys had it easy—the whole cabin was in on it. How would she sneak her bags past all those girls?

And what if something bad happened to her all the way over there? Something bad, and he wouldn't be there to help her.

She'll come, she'll make it, don't worry, she's okay, she's fine.

They crept along the final remnants of the path until it merged into grass and a bit of undergrowth. Wesley led the way with his flashlight; he almost started to whistle then he held his tongue. Even the slightest things might risk the plan. It was tricky, but it would work—they'd cut through here to the road, then travel uphill. Al had a map and they'd follow it to the bus station a few miles ahead. They'd take the bus with what little money they had and get home, and by the time the counselors discovered that the kids were nowhere to be found, each of them would be explaining it to their parents.

On paper, it was perfect.

But things never go as planned.

Wendy showed up around eleven-ten and apologized for being late. She didn't have a single bag with her besides her purse, and said it would've been impossible to pack two suitcases with all those other girls around.

Wesley led them through the dark tangled woods. Every shadow became The Raven Hill Butcher. Every shadow was his arm, every shadow was his knife, and every shadow threatened to pull them in to their death and demise.

"Is—is it far?" Ralph asked.

"No, not very far," Wesley said. "We'll be there soon."

From the right came footsteps; the group stopped. Through the night, they all looked at each other, eyes darting, wondering who the stranger with them was. The distant person was silent for a while—frozen—then the footsteps started up again. It was coming from the direction they intended to travel.

"Who—who's there?"

"Shush." Wendy whispered.

The noises stopped again.

"Must've been an animal," Al said.

"I hope you're right," Wesley said.

The group moved past low branches and swatted mosquitos. Night thickened; night consumed them. The darkness was claustrophobic.

"Now through here," Wesley said lower than a whisper, "towards the right a little ways we'll find a path. A clearing. We—"

Ralph tripped on something, bumped into Wesley's back, and both boys crashed into a tree. Pain raced up Wesley's body. He was so angry at Ralph he could've smacked him.

"Sorry," Ralph said after catching his breath. "I slipped on something."

Wendy lent Wesley a hand. "You okay?"

"Yeah, thanks."

Al and Bill offered hands to Ralph but he didn't take them. He was staring at something between his feet.

RETURN TO CAMP SOLGOHACHIA

"Ralph?" Al said. "Come on dammit let's go."

Wesley shined his light on Ralph's body then dragged it between his legs and to his feet to reveal the severed foot of a man being picked at by bugs. Veins hung over the sides and the jagged edges of bone tore through a layer of flesh.

Wesley moved the light away quickly. Ralph screamed at the top of his lungs, so Al put his hands around his mouth to mask it.

"Shut up."

"Oh God," Wendy said. "Whose could that be?"

The boys gave each other a look as if they knew. Then, at the same time, Wesley, Al, and Bill whispered, "Vince?"

It was no longer footsteps from the distance to their right, but full-fledged running. Someone was rushing to get them.

The kids scrambled away from the sound—Wesley didn't know what waited in the other side of these woods. Everybody had gone their own direction, completely avoiding whoever was running at them from their intended destination.

Wesley was all alone and pressed his body against a tree. Down below him he heard footsteps. People running and hiding in every direction.

He peeked around the tree to see a figure ten or twelve feet below him towering over Ralph. Ralph cried, threw his hands over his face, staggered backwards, then the figure—The Raven Hill Butcher—put his hands around Ralph and raised him into the air. He knocked Ralph back and forth and Ralph screamed as loud as thunder. The Raven Hill Butcher raised Ralph and slammed his neck into a six-inch thick tree branch. Ralph's head split off his body.

NASSER RABADI

Wesley couldn't control his own screams and dropped his flashlight in shock.

The light was still on and signaled The Raven Hill Butcher to his location; for a moment it shined across the monster's face and Wesley swore that even though light touched it, the man was still as dark as a funeral scarf.

Wesley reached to pick it up then changed his mind—The Butcher was after him.

Wesley moved faster and harder than he had done during the race with Bill. His heart palpitated and his hands were slick with sweat. He pictured Ralph's head falling to the ground like a pencil falling off a table.

Al shrieked somewhere far away; he screamed when he found Ralph—Wesley could hear it even over the rustling leaves below his feet and the killer's.

It took him a while to realize the killer's footsteps had stopped. Wesley flinched when he turned around to see darkness. He wondered if the killer—if The Raven Hill Butcher—was hidden in pure darkness, becoming one with it, and was ready to grab him and decapitate him too. He wondered if The Butcher could move through shadows, teleporting from one shadow to the next, and was going to come up from the ground and slash his legs open.

Footsteps suddenly came from behind Wesley; he turned around, ready to fight somehow.

It wasn't The Butcher; it was Wendy.

"We're gonna die," she whispered then hugged him, her face full of tears. "We're all gonna die, aren't we? We're all gonna die."

RETURN TO CAMP SOLGOHACHIA

He hugged her back and ran a hand through her hair. "No, no, we are not dying. Come on. We need to find Bill and Al. We need to get out of here."

"He's gonna kill us."

"Shush. No he's not. Come on, Wendy."

He held her hand and they cautiously tiptoed back the way he was originally running from, the way that they were originally meant to go. He took deep breaths, bravely leading her, and looked furtively for the others or for The Raven Hill Butcher.

They hid behind a tree, looked in every direction, then paced to another one.

Al's cries started again, and with the cries came footsteps.

The Raven Hill Butcher came forward down the slope and raised his knife, then cocked his head to the side.

Wesley and Wendy held each other, looking down at him slithering closer to Al. Wesley wanted to yell, but that'd be a dead giveaway. He prayed Bill was safe somewhere, maybe he had made it back to the road, maybe he was running and running and going to make it home.

Again he felt the urge to yell. He didn't know what they could do, but they had to do something, didn't they?

"Let's run," Wendy whispered. "Let's go—ohmigod."

NASSER RABADI

Wesley was fixated on Al and The Butcher; The Butcher came within five feet of Al, and Wesley finally screamed—he couldn't help it. *"Al watch out."*

The Raven Hill Butcher did not acknowledge his shouts.

Wesley was ready to run with Wendy but couldn't leave without Bill—it might've been too late for Al, but Bill was a brother to him. He was his friend—his best friend, he couldn't leave him alone in the forest to die. Maybe he had made it to the road already and wasn't still here—but Wesley needed to know for sure.

Al faced The Raven Hill Butcher. *"I'm gonna kill you."*

Then Al raised his knife and charged, aiming for the throat, and came within inches of it; The Butcher grabbed him at the wrist and twisted it around all the way backwards; Wesley heard it snap through Al's screams of pain. With his other hand, he tried to punch The Butcher—tried to do something, anything—then The Butcher brought his blade up from his side and severed Al's other hand.

The Butcher grabbed Al by the hair, then split his head open on a tree. Brains oozed from the crack; blood gushed like a fountain.

Immediately, he turned straight around to face Wesley and Wendy. The pair looked at each other and screamed. Hand in hand they ran, and The Raven Hill Butcher chased. He moved with an elegance—with a knowledge of where every branch and root in the woods was. Where everything in the woods was. And when Wesley and Wendy ran, they had to dodge many crooked branches and winding roots and it slowed them down. Wesley glanced over his shoulder…

…The Butcher was near.

RETURN TO CAMP SOLGOHACHIA

Wendy was tired and slowing them down—their hands were sliding away from each other. She was two feet behind Wesley, and he tried to pull her forward when The Raven Hill Butcher grabbed her first. He yanked on her hair and pulled her body into his arms; he set his dirty blade to her throat and she wailed uncontrollably.

The first incision was small, and as he started to pull it across her squirming body, he collapsed.

Bill grabbed onto the killer's torso, brough him to the ground clutching Al's knife—Wesley couldn't imagine prying that from a dead man's hands—and buried it in The Butcher's neck. The Butcher let go of Wendy and reached for Bill.

"Go." Bill screamed. *"Go now."*

"We can't leave you."

Wendy pulled on Wesley, trying to pull him with her into the woods.

"Go."

Wesley listened to Bill; he ran away with Wendy.

They ran to the road and never stopped, even when they heard his footsteps behind them.

From the road, they ran for miles to the bus stop, and even when they arrived back to their homes…

…they still heard him running behind them.

NASSER RABADI

In a heart-pounding thriller, aspiring actress Samantha Monroe becomes a witness to murder, entangling herself with a deadly hitman named Tom, and together, they must navigate a perilous conspiracy, where danger lurks at every turn.

READ THE "AFTERLIFE" SERIES OF PSYCHOLOGICAL THRILLERS FOR FREE ON kindle unlimited

available at amazon

AUTHOR'S NOTES

I had never written a camp story before but I love them. Some of my favorite *Goosebumps* books were set at camps, and some of my favorite slasher flicks like *The Burning* and *Sleepaway Camp* franchiseand *Friday The Thirteenth* franchise were set at camps, so I figured why not set this prequel at one.

It was very challenging to write in a camp setting since I had never previously done so, but it was fun. One thing you must always do as a writer or any sort of creative/artist is to challenge yourself and step out of your comfort zone. So I did. And I had fun. Maybe I've got another camp story in me somewhere.

This was an interesting prequel to write, and originally I thought I'd focus more so on The Raven Hill Butcher's origin, but as I went on writing, I felt it would be better placed in another book. So we *definitely* have more of his origin coming. And we have not seen the last of Camp Solgohachia.

I hope you all liked this book, and don't forget to check out the rest of the *Raven Hill Butcher* series.

The rest of the series can be found here: https://www.amazon.com/dp/B0BQKVH3Z6

NASSER RABADI

If you want to stay up to date make sure to follow me on Twitter and Instagram and YouTube.

https://twitter.com/nasserrabadi13

https://www.instagram.com/nasserrabadi13/

https://www.youtube.com/nasserrabadi

You can also join my newsletter at https://mailchi.mp/3b31e29016d9/nasser

And please check out my other books such as the *Engstrom House* trilogy: https://www.amazon.com/dp/B0BG3SHSX4

I am also on Patreon where you can get previews (and even commentary) of my upcoming books before they hit Amazon and Kindle https://www.patreon.com/NasserRabadi13

RETURN TO CAMP SOLGOHACHIA

Thanks again everybody! If you enjoyed Return to Camp Solgohachia please leave a review. Word of mouth is the best way to help independent authors, so if you have a friend who might enjoy this series, please let them know. I really appreciate it, and I hope you enjoyed camp with Wesley and his buddies!

Chapter Eleven
BONUS CONTENT!

Specially included in this new edition of Return to Camp Solgo-hachia are two previews for you! The first is a preview of the next book in this series, Noel Hell. The second preview is for the opening chapter of The Haunting of Engstrom House, which is the first book in the Engstrom House trilogy.

If you enjoy the preview chapters, you can order Return to Noel Hell (and the rest of this series) here: https://www.amazon.com/dp/B0BQKVH3Z6

And you can order the Engstrom House trilogy here: https://www.amazon.com/dp/B0BG3SHSX4

Chapter Twelve

NOEL HELL CHAPTER ONE

THE RAVEN HILL BUTCHER BOOK THREE

T he world became a snow globe.

With the drifts of snow came rumors plentifully. Nobody in the dreadful town of Raven Hill would forget the previous winter's massacre. Of course, Raven Hill hadn't always been dreadful. It used to be quiet—it used to be a place where people were happy. But something had changed all of that, something had come to Raven Hill with a demented, twisted, overbearing presence. It passed through almost unnoticed, but soon took its form in the minds of Raven Hill's residents, mostly the children, and came to life.

Whispers escaped the lips of locals, wondering if the horrors which befell them the year previous would return, or if the horrors had wandered to another place on earth. But that was foolish to think that the horrors were over, for horror still brooded heavily with bat wings over the homes of Raven Hill. Any of them could be next—somebody had to be.

Panic hadn't been this blatant in Raven Hill since the butchering of two girls in the earlier 70s. With another massacre, the slayings at Camp Solgohachia which occurred a few years prior at the border between Raven Hill and Carpentersville, more hysteria was rising.

The holiday spirits were almost entirely absent this year; the words *He sees you when you're sleeping, he knows when you're awake,* took on a new meaning, and the residents did watch out.

Christmas decorations were abundant and decorated Raven Hill from head to toe, but it did not feel like Christmas. It did not feel peaceful. It did not feel merry and bright. No matter how much snow fell, it couldn't return that joy that had been stripped from the town. For now, troubles would not be out of sight.

It snowed, and snowed, and snowed.

Last year was the only other time it had snowed this generously.

One whispered to the other, "Do you think it's really over?"

And the other whispered back, watching the snowflakes tumble blindly, "I hope so."

But both of them knew it was nowhere near over.

The van skidded a little, but Jill had it under control. The roads had been cleared a little while ago, but as snowfall resumed, the once empty streets filled monstrously with mountains of deathly white snow. It was warm in the van and bright outside, but now drafts of cold slithered in serpent-like and caressed Jill Lawler and her little sister Emma Lawler. It was early in the day and they were both excited for their winter getaway with their friends—a weekend away from everybody, they'd be headed to the Asylum Resort. It looked beautiful in all the pictures Jill had seen. There'd be a pool, a nice bar, comfy beds. Who could ask for more? She smiled thinking about it, turned off the highway exit, and continued straight down the road where acres of farmland surrounded either side. It was a different part of Raven Hill—a quieter part, a part that Jill had picked because it was far away from where that massacre happened a year ago, and she was terrified of it.

Massacre. Thinking of the word made her shudder.

Jill glanced at her sister; Emma was staring through the window, watching the snowflakes, unaware she was tapping her fingers against the glass. *Have Yourself A Merry Little Christmas* came through the radio, and Jill sang along. Next came *White Christmas.* It was nice to get into the Christmas mood, it was nice to feel happy. It hadn't seemed like Christmas in a long, long time.

I wonder if it'll ever feel like Christmas again, Jill thought. *After high school it stopped feeling like that holiday feeling for* everything.

Emma finally turned away from the windows. "What movies did you bring?"

"Back to the Future and *Heathers."*

Emma smiled. "I love Heathers."

"Then answer this," Jill said. "You inherit five million dollars but the same day, aliens land on earth and say they're going to blow it up in two days. What do you do?"

97

"Probably buy enough food to feed the homeless. I can't see it going to much use any other way."

"Totally. At least if they blew up earth I wouldn't have to worry about student loans or credit card debt," Jill said. "I'd probably... I wouldn't do anything with it. Might as well spend the last two days with family and friends. Play Monopoly or something."

"Great, Jill, you'd convince everyone you love to hate you in the last two days of existence."

"Okay Ems. Maybe I'd buy a million dogs and cuddle with them before aliens blow up our planet."

"Woah, that's a lot better than what I said. I'd rather inherit a million dogs than that money."

"Now let's not get too crazy, I'd much rather have the money if the impending doom isn't coming."

"Nope. Doom or no doom," Emma said, "I'd choose a million dogs over five million dollars."

"You're crazy."

"I know."

When they were thirty minutes away black clouds covered the sun, and snow gushed from the sky. The brightness that had previously filled the morning evaporated, and they were left with a hollow shell of how cheerful the day had looked. It was as if someone had placed a black and white filter over earth. Loud gusts of wind banged against the car as it passed over the winding road. Jill wondered how much snow they could possibly be buried in before they reached the hotel.

"Insane, isn't it?"

"Yeah."

RETURN TO CAMP SOLGOHACHIA

"It's those darn clouds."

Jill grew nervous; she was never superstitious like her sister was, but the dark clouds seemed like an omen. Her hands tightened around the steering wheel, her foot pressed harder on the gas, then she turned on her headlights and scanned the road up ahead. Suddenly she was remembering all of the hellish ghost stories she had read as a little girl about drivers who would see ghosts as they passed through certain areas, unaware that the road or nearby building was haunted. Sometimes these ghosts would appear as hitchhikers, and the drivers would pick them up and be slaughtered—and Jill never intended ever in her life to pick up a hitchhiker since reading those stories. Jill thought of the Hobb's End Ghost in Maine, where a woman dressed in a Victorian-era gown traverses the streets, and cars are sometimes seen passing through her. Then there was the story of another lady, in a town she couldn't quite recall, whose car blew its engine on an interstate, and who claimed, in reverse of these typical stories, that a ghost had given *her* a ride in a truck.

There's no such thing as ghosts, she thought, but a morbid premonition came anyways. It was followed by a chill slithering through her spine. The back of her skull itched—an image flashed in her mind's eye. A shadow at first, a blanket of darkness. Then, through it, emerged a dull glimmer reflecting an unseen light. Slowly, the shadow took form into that of a man holding a knife set in aged wood. Jill was clueless as to where that hellish image came from, but it felt real—as real as the wheel that she gripped so forcefully that it made the palms of her hands white.

NASSER RABADI

Snow was coming down heavier now and the draft of cold chilled her, but no matter how cold snow could make her, the chill she received from her premonition was always colder.

Suddenly, as she loosened her grip on the wheel, she was flooded with a feeling of danger. For a minute she froze with a rigidness that was not natural. It had never happened to Jill like that before—it was worse than a premonition.

Jill glanced at herself in the rearview mirror and saw that she had gone pale—as pale as a plucked flower. Then she looked at Emma and saw she was asleep. She wondered what her sister was dreaming about.

Now they were only about ten minutes away from the Asylum Resort—what a time for Emma to sleep. Jill laughed. Her lips pulled into a smile when she thought about the pool and the hot tub of the hotel, and how relaxing it would be to take a swim then return to the hotel room for a movie and drinks. She wondered how long it would take the others to arrive, and if they'd be mad if she went swimming without them—the others were arriving later, and Jill and Emma would be early.

No, there'd be no harm in taking an early swim.

Jill became lost in her thoughts and almost missed the Asylum Resort when it came up on the right. Quickly she turned off the road and into the parking lot that was an ocean of snow. There were only two other cars.

She shook Emma awake, turned off the engine, and the girls grabbed their things.

RETURN TO CAMP SOLGOHACHIA

The hotel looked nothing like it did in its photos, which must've been taken at a more pleasant time than now. The hotel was tattered and it wore its discolored brown bricks proudly. Even the glass doors seemed lackluster; there was no shine to it at all. The Asylum Resort looked miserable. It had been converted out of an old warehouse and seemed to still carry all of the warehouse's depressing features of abandonment. But the hotel was not abandoned; there were workers seen walking past the front doors.

Emma was disgusted. *"This is the place you picked out?"*

"Trust me, it looked amazing in the pictures."

The girls walked awkwardly through the piling snow, and checked in with the receptionist. She smelled of stale perfume and the girls realized that this was not the kind of hotel they'd like to stay in, but they were already here and had a room reserved and their friends were already on their way. The tables in the lobby had ashtrays instead of flowers, and the fur rug below their feet that covered golden wooden panels needed to be replaced since 1962.

After checking in and getting the keys for room 429, they went on the elevator and Jill pushed the button for the fourth floor. The hotel didn't have those giant carts for fitting all of their bags on, and Jill was regretting picking this place.

"What a trash place this is," Emma said. "There's not even a cart for our bags."

"I'm sorry," Jill said. "God, I should've done research on this place. Hotels are *always* nicer in the pictures aren't they?"

"I guess we'll be fine as long as they have a pool and hot tub. At this point I'd settle for just *one* of those two."

NASSER RABADI

The elevator made a *PING!* when it came to the fourth floor and the metal doors slid open and let them into the hallway. It was long, blue, and formed into a plus sign at the intersection. In all there were four hallways on the fourth floor. It seemed nicer up here—so far, at least—than in the lobby. Here there were no signs of nasty ashtrays, and the carpets didn't look terribly old and smelly. Waves of the ocean were painted on the walls, and fake candles placed over old gothic candleholders lit the halls.

"Not so bad up here, is it?" Jill asked.

"The room'll be the ultimate test."

"It's so quiet in here. Have you seen anybody else around, Ems?"

"No, but there were so few cars in the parking lot and it seemed like most if not all of the keys were behind that receptionist. The others should be in 430."

The rooms outside of the elevator started with 400 on the right and 401 on the left. In the middle of the hallway, where it turned into a plus sign, they made a right. The numbers continued to increase, starting with 420 on the right and 421 on the left. Each segment of the long hallways had about twenty rooms. Halfway down they came to room 429 and slipped in the key.

The door sealed behind them on its own with a hiss. Coldness crept against their bodies; the curtains fluttered on the wall opposite of them and just for a moment—maybe less—Jill could have sworn she saw legs behind them. But that couldn't have been.

She rubbed her eyes, went forward across the brown carpeted floor, and shut the windows. It was a miracle there was no snow in the room, and she wondered how that could be. It was almost as if...
It hadn't been open until now.

RETURN TO CAMP SOLGOHACHIA

"Should we say something to management?" Emma asked.

"No," Jill said nervously. "It's not that cold. Let's just crank the heat up."

Jill turned the dial on the thermostat and put the temperature to eighty degrees. It had been on seventy beforehand.

The room was cozy; two twin beds cramped on either side of a nightstand, a television on a dresser across from them, and a mini fridge and a coffee maker next to the sink outside of the bathroom near the entrance. There was no balcony, but the windows provided a view of the street and the parking lot.

Snow came down reminiscent of last year's winter. The girls stood together and watched it. With it came dreadful feelings for Jill, whose lips had pulled into a grimace. It had never snowed this much in Raven Hill until last year and she wondered why it was doing it again now. She thought about those girls who were snowed in last year... snowed in and killed. Jill saw that her own reflection was pale—pale as the angel of a grave.

"It reminds me of it too," Emma said.

Jill turned away from it quickly. "We should check out that pool."

"You sure they have it?"

"We passed it on the first floor, didn't you see?"

Emma shrugged. "Can't be too careful with this hellhole hotel. That's what they should rename it, instead of Asylum Resort, the Hellhole Resort."

Jill opened her suitcase and moved things around until she found her bathing suit, then changed into it and grabbed a towel that she tied around herself. Even though the hotel seemed deserted save for the staff, she always felt as if she were naked and all eyes were on her when she went through the hallways of hotels in a bathing suit—even if it were a modest one-piece and covered most of her midriff. She put on her flipflops, and after she and Emma changed, they went by room 430 just to check if their friends had arrived yet. They were sure that they hadn't, but it didn't hurt to check, so Jill knocked on the door.

No answer.

The girls went down the elevator, arrived on the main floor, and went to the pool room.

The pool was about twenty feet in length and no deeper than four feet. The floor of ugly square tiles was already soaking wet, which was odd, since as far as they could see there were no other guests swimming. Large windows lined the walls and snow brimmed to their bases and was still coming down hard. There was a hot tub in the corner, and Emma ran straight towards it and jumped in—which was against the no diving sign that hung above it.

Jill laughed then came over to the hot tub stairs and walked down them when Emma pulled her in. the water gave Jill a soothing burn and for a while, all problems were gone from her mind.

He watched them.

He peered through the window; he was ready for them.

Oh, he was ready for them.

He felt their fears radiating like a blazing fire.

His hand wrapped tightly around the blade set in aging wood.

RETURN TO CAMP SOLGOHACHIA

Then he disappeared.

Chapter Thirteen

THE HAUNTING OF ENGSTROM HOUSE CHAPTER ONE

ENGSTROM HOUSE BOOK ONE

Engstrom House was under constant shadow, as if sunlight could not reach past its gate on its hill in Ashfall. Its windows—oversized, divided into many parts, and always shut—were always black. Stunted sickly trees grew prolifically in the forest behind it, and tangled vegetation was abundant at the house's sides.

Engstrom House was uninhabited for many years; its previous owners, who lived as recluses, and whose doors were seldom disturbed by the knock of any visitor, had disappeared. When the trouble began, it began slowly—soft knocks in the deep hours of night that gradually became frequent. Creeping unseen footsteps in all levels of the house. Moonlight shined through a window and rolled out in long stretches; the little boy who was looking over from his bed saw a silhouetted figure pass through the glow. On each occasion investigation revealed nothing, and all occurrences were ascribed to imagination alone.

There were curious whispers and rumors of ghouls seen around Engstrom House; figures that were seldom completely human, but often approaching humanity in varying degree. Most of the creatures were forward slumping with glaring red eyes. Some were nameless blasphemies with sharp horns that curved inward toward each other, bat wings whose beating made no noise, and ugly prehensile claws.

It was said that Engstrom House's trees swayed ominously at night, and it was swore that they did so even when there was no wind, and that was said too of the misshapen weeds in the high terraced yard where birds never lingered.

In town there were odd conversations about what abnormal things had been seen or felt near Engstrom House; while it stood alone on its hill, people were careful never to pass by it. And it would not take long before travelers passing through Ashfall heard of things locked in the attic, and of strange amorphous shadows glimpsed in windows at all levels.

Everything that happened in Engstrom House's wide staircases, long eternally dark passages, and hidden doors in unusual corners is unknown. Cold wind chilled those who stood afar and watched the house; did something still walk its halls?

Within two years of Engstrom House's completion, every person in the Engstrom family was dead. The Engstrom children died of mysterious sicknesses. Body parts—but almost never whole bod-

RETURN TO CAMP SOLGOHACHIA

ies—of missing adults were discovered, and servants told incredible tales of voices and ominous sounds heard in walls and whispers they swore came from empty rooms.

Exactly one month after Engstrom House was completed, the youngest boy in the Engstrom family fell from the rooftop. He was found by a servant who told the family that John Engstrom had been pushed and had not fallen accidentally—but pushed by whom, the servant could not say. The same servant went missing before John's funeral.

A few months later, Helen Engstrom, the oldest of the Engstrom children, went up a staircase at night to find an extra blanket for one of her sisters. While Helen's footsteps were heard all the way to the storage closet and back to the stairs, she was never seen again. Sometimes, it was said, her footsteps still echoed the halls.

Agatha was the first of the Engstrom children to die of sickness. Each child had different symptoms. Agatha suffered from dizziness which became so severe that she could not stand, and after putting up a desperate fight for three and a half weeks, she passed away in her sleep. Joyce suffered from an intense cough that caused her to spit up blood; Joyce died several months after Agatha, and when the doctors examined her corpse, they found maggots eating her lungs.

Timothy became ill one year after Agatha's passing, and was stuck in bed with what seemed to be a cold. He was only in bed for a few days, but as he was on the brink of recovery, he felt sharp pain pulsing in the back of his head. He was dead less than a day later. When the family's doctor examined Timothy's corpse, there was half of a needle stuck in the back of his skull; while it could not be determined if he passed away from the sickness or from the broken

109

needle, nobody could be sure how the needle was put in his head in the first place.

Rapidly approaching the two year anniversary, the only remaining Engstrom child—Thaddeus—went mad, uttering shrieking horrors and screaming all through the night that he was not Thaddeus and did not belong in the house. Thaddeus screamed about unseen things in the air which he could not describe; something was fastening itself onto him that ought not to be. He screamed that nothing was ever still in the night—the walls and shadows shifted, things moved and changed and fluttered. The best doctors in Ashfall treated him, and for a while, it was suggested that he should be taken to Piedmont Wellness, a hospital in the neighboring town, but he died before that could be arranged.

Mrs. Engstrom starved herself to death. Her shriveled body was found collapsed at the base of the hill. The following day her husband vanished without a trace, and three months later Mr. Engstrom's dismembered corpse was found in only a few pieces scattered through unused rooms on every floor in Engstrom House. Nobody was charged with his murder.

The Bloch family moved in two decades after the Engstrom family's demise. There were eight of them: Mr. Bloch, his wife, his father, his three sons, and his two daughters. No member of the Bloch family was ever found.

The Bloch children told their friends of things they had heard or seen in all corners and levels of the house, and told about odd occurrences that happened in all hours of night. Sometimes they spoke of eyes at the bottom of stairways, or footsteps heard in halls. There had even been curious whispers about nightmarishly misshapen faces seen in dreams.

Just before the Bloch family had gone missing, Mrs. Bloch had given strange warnings to her relatives about the house. She had told friends in town that there were things in that house beyond any human understanding; things that were wholly unknown and indescribable to mankind.

When it was discovered that the Bloch family had gone missing, an investigation lasting one year was launched into their whereabouts. Nothing had been stolen from their home, and no trace of them was discovered in any neighboring town—all towns within a thirty mile radius were checked.

All that remained of the Bloch family was a single note in Mr. Bloch's handwriting, found in the pocket of one of his shirts. In hurried handwriting, it read: *I hear them in the walls, and I'm going to look for them.*

In Mr. Bloch's journal—of which several pages had been mysteriously torn and lost, and several remaining pages toward the end were entirely indecipherable—there were more references to voices and sounds hidden in walls. One such entry read: *I followed it for the first time today—that old familiar voice. I couldn't take more of the mystery, so I followed it. It's been on my mind every minute of every day. That little voice in the walls. I thought if I opened the wall I'd find it—whoever it really is—but there was nothing behind the portion of wall I broke open.*

Another entry in the journal recounted a dream of his: *The oaken door had fallen, and there I found a terrible row of ten stone cells with rusty bars. Three had tenants, all skeletons of very high grade, and on the bony forefinger of one I found a seal ring with unusual symbols carved into it. At the end of the cells I found a crypt with cases of formally arranged bones, some of them bearing terrible parallel inscriptions carved in Latin and Greek.*

In a prehistoric tumuli I brought to light skulls which were slightly more human than a gorilla's, and which bore indescribable ideographic carvings. Suddenly I found myself in a midnight cavern of boundless depth where no ray of light could penetrate. We will never know what sightless stygian worlds lay beyond the little distance I went.

After the Bloch family disappeared, their heirs kept the grass cut and took care of the garden; they did renovations in hopes that they could sell the house and pass on its curse to the next owner, whoever that may be.

The house never sold.

All of these years later, its creaking floors were never walked again by any permanent guests. Perhaps only spiders lived there now, and so many generations have gone by so that the spiders thought they had been the ones to build Engstrom House.

Dull and quiet, Engstrom House rested alone, and Ashfall children dared each other to go near its fence, unaware of its history that echoed within the walls. Somewhere inside was left the imprint of its many, many lives long lost and long forgotten, so that even the names of all the deceased were not known.

While most of what happened there was mystery, and would forever be unknown, there was one thing that everyone generally believed: that Engstrom House was *not* empty, that something unnatural was inside of it. Where the evilness had originated from would only be speculation. What caused all that trouble so long ago would all be a guess. The history of the house revealed no trace of the sinister either about its construction, or about the family who built it.

In the dead of night, formless shadows passed by Engstrom House's deepest window seats; Engstrom House watched every move that the sleeping town of Ashfall made. Unknown things stirred in empty halls and empty hidden doorways. Spiders crawled wickedly and freely up and down walls and beds; coldness spread through lonely rooms.

Engstrom House was alive tonight, because it knew that soon somebody would be visiting.

Printed in Great Britain
by Amazon

50058916R00067